"As for you, Eric," the Krith said carefully, "we are not yet certain *what* you are—*or what you have become.*"

He stepped closer to Eric's motionless figure. Two bodyguards flanked the Krith, the aim of their weapons never faltering.

"You cannot harm us, neither you nor your Shadowy Man." The Krith nodded to the two gunmen, who turned away. "Because we know about your physical condition—and its relationship to your, ah, replicas."

The Krith's voice was interrupted by the remote chattering of automatic weapons, the sounds of shattering glass and spilling liquids.

Even while fingers were pulling back on triggers, Eric felt himself dying, dissolving, as leaden slugs tore through the bodies of his helpless, cloned replicas. He felt the horrible agonies of their dying, *a prelude to his own...*

VESTIGES
OF TIME

RICHARD C. MEREDITH
THE TIMELINER TRILOGY
BOOK THREE

PLAYBOY PRESS
PAPERBACKS

CONTENTS

1

The Slums of VarKhohs

The late afternoon sun should have been brighter and warmer than it was, for it had been a late summer day in the city of VarKhohs. But now the light seemed dim and cold, as if from an aged, weakened sun, as it fell into the dark and narrow streets through which I slowly followed a man I knew by the name RyoNa. Although he was still several blocks ahead of me, I could easily make him out, a large, heavy man in a rich, dark robe, one decorated with the symbols of his rank and caste, a man seemingly very out of place in the slums into which he had led me.

I tried to throw off the gloom that settled over me as I followed him farther into the decaying slums, past the ramshackle buildings that filled the quarter of the city nearest the river. I pulled my own robe more tightly around me against the imaginary chill, a robe not so dark or so regal as that of RyoNa; but then I wasn't trying to appear to be a member of one of the ruling castes of NakrehVatee, the nation and society that dominated North America in the summer of A.D. 1972 on this *particular* Earth. I was just trying to get by until I could get my hands on what I had come so far across the Lines of Time to find. And I thought RyoNa could help me find what I wanted: a "time machine." In a sense, it turned out that he was helping me do that, although he didn't know it at the time, and I couldn't have guessed just what that "time machine" was to be.

RyoNa turned a corner ahead of me, passing in front of a temple dedicated to one of the Dark Lords of

Death, the god Themfo-Okketho, by name, and for a moment he was lost from my view. I hurried forward a little more quickly, as quickly as the folds of the robe around me would allow, and placed a hand on the comforting bulge of an energy pistol under my left armpit. I wouldn't have felt very comfortable in *that* section of the city without a weapon. I hadn't been in VarKhohs long, but I'd been there long enough to have heard tales of what took place in those slums after dark, of what happened to well-dressed men and women foolish enough to be down there after daylight had gone and there was no longer even a pretense of police protection.

Finally I reached the corner where I'd seen RyoNa turn, and as I rounded the corner myself, passing through the shadow cast by the statue of the hideous deathgod, I saw RyoNa's bulky figure, not as far away as it had been. Apparently he had slowed to make certain he didn't lose me. He knew I was following him, of course. Only I wasn't certain whether he knew that I knew of his awareness. Our understanding was a rather tacit one, if it could be called an understanding at all.

A small, ragged child, who had been standing in the open doorway of one of the crumbling buildings of gray stone and cracked brick, made a motion as if to accost me, perhaps to ask for a handout, or, equally likely, pimping for his mother or sister, but I held him off with a curt shake of my head, a hard look from my eyes. I'd never been what you'd call handsome, and the events of the past year or so had done nothing to improve my looks: I have an especially unpleasant-looking scar on my right cheek where it once was opened to the bone by a pistol barrel. I guess my face was enough for the poor urchin. He went back into his doorway. Silently I wished him well, knowing how unlikely his well-being in this world was.

There were a few others in the streets of the slums

of VarKhohs, other tatter-clad children like the boy in the doorway, male and female alike dressed in the sexless rags of poverty, and there were adults as well, weary, disillusioned—if they'd ever had illusions—old before their time, too far down the ladder of this world's society to concern themselves with the badges of their caste. When you're that far down, it doesn't much matter, except perhaps in the ingrown subcultures and the jealously guarded pecking orders that must exist even for the lowest.

The poverty wasn't all that new to me. I'd experienced conditions as bad, and even worse, in dozens of other cities of the parallel worlds of time. I didn't like it, but I'd grown accustomed to it. Yet . . . what did disturb me about the poverty of the people of the slums of VarKhohs was its total lack of reason. The poverty wasn't necessary!

Only a few miles from the streets through which I followed RyoNa stood the wealthy center of one of the most highly developed civilizations I'd ever seen. It was a culture based on the technologies of nuclear fusion and plasma physics, a civilization with the wealth to send fleets of starships to Alpha Centauri and Tau Ceti, where human colonies flourished, with the wealth to build the shining, shimmering towers in which the upper castes of VarKhohs dwelt, soaring penthouses that seemed to reach the clouds and from the windows of which one could look out across the ocean and see the sleek yachts moving between the luxurious artificial islands that floated a few miles offshore, with the wealth to construct tombs in the southwestern deserts for its rulers that made the most lavish of those of ancient Egypt look cheap and mean by comparison. This civilization had the affluence to allow a select few of its members to live—and die!—in luxury such as human beings had seldom known before but didn't have the wealth—or rather the desire—to give a decent meal to those who stooped at the bottom of the social pyramid under the crushing weight of all those who stood above.

Eric Mathers, I suddenly found myself asking silently, where in Hades did you ever develop a social conscience? And I didn't have an answer for that one, nor really the time to speculate about it. I had something to do that I felt was even more important than concern over the lower classes of VarKhohs. I had to find the Shadowy Man. And that probably would require a time machine.

The man I knew as RyoNa had slowed a little more, allowing me to come nearer to him, and then turned down a still darker, narrower street, no more than an alley. I moved after him and reached the entrance of the alley in time to see him entering a large, open doorway and pause in the deeper shadows there as if to make certain I was still with him.

I entered the alley, glanced back down the street from which I had come, and saw the statue of Themfo-Okketho, the deathgod, silhouetted against the deepening afternoon sky. For some reason it sent a chill through me and brought to mind an old phrase about someone stepping on my grave. I tried to ignore it and went on into the alley.

Now there seemed to be no one else around. Just RyoNa and me. So maybe it was time I caught up with him and finally spoke to him. We'd played this silly game long enough. Now I'd like to hear him say in no uncertain terms that he could get me one of the so-called chronal-displacement devices—a machine that allegedly could travel not horizontally across the Lines of Time from parallel Earth to parallel Earth, as does a skudder, but forward and backward in time, into the future and into the past—in short, a "time machine," as one writer had long ago dubbed such a machine, but on an Earth very different from this one.

And maybe, I thought, RyoNa had decided on the

same thing, for he still seemed to be waiting for me just inside the large doorway.

As I reached the doorway, RyoNa took a few steps backward into the darker interior and then spoke a word that I couldn't make out, for it was hardly more than a whisper and, as it turned out, not directed toward me at all.

I could hardly make them out at first, those who came from even farther back in the darkness, several of them, men as big as RyoNa or even bigger, and more given to muscle than the plump, well-groomed man I'd been following. And I knew they weren't jumping out to bid me good evening and welcome to their humble abode.

As I stepped backward, trying to gain the advantage of what little light there was in the alley, I did two things: externally, my right hand made its way through the folds of the robe I wore and found the butt of the energy pistol I'd been carrying in case something like this did happen; internally, I switched my body into combat augmentation. The world around me seemed to slow down; sounds dopplered toward the bass registers; what light I could see seemed to shift toward the red end of the spectrum; and certain rods and cones of my eyes allowed me to perceive more of what was taking place in the shadows of the alley as they electronically shifted into lower-light modes.

The pistol was now free of the robe, and I brought it up, clicking off the safety, trying to get it up in time to fire, though even with augmentation coming into operation I wasn't fast enough for that.

In the moments I had left, I could see that there were six of them, as big as I'd thought, all clad in black, and with furious determination written on their faces. What kind of men were these that RyoNa had sent at me? And why had he done it? Then there was no more time for speculation. . . .

An expertly swung, heavily booted foot came up

and knocked the energy pistol from my hand, for an instant stunning my right arm, but by that time I'd come up to full X5 and was able to lash back at the man before his foot was on the ground again. My half-numbed, half-stinging hand was balled into a fist that must have loosened a few teeth and may have broken a nose as it skidded across his face. I didn't have time to check. The rest of them were on me.

I think I gave a pretty good account of myself, all things considered, but there were six of them—now five, then four—but even with the advantages of augmentation, I'm no superman. While I was tangling with three of them, one having somehow latched on to my left arm with a grip I couldn't break, the fourth got behind me and did his damnedest to break open my skull with something very heavy and very blunt. He came too close to succeeding for my comfort.

I was only half-aware of the sensation that knocked my head forward, brought a flash of lightning to my eyes, and robbed me of all ability to direct the actions of my hands and feet. I went limp and felt my augmentation automatically cutting itself out. I held on to consciousness for only a few seconds longer, just long enough to hear the voice of RyoNa, who came closer to me now, speaking EKhona, the language of this part of the local world. "I didn't expect you to put up such a great fight, Harkos. I am astonished at your prowess. You *are* the man we're looking for, I'm certain. Welcome, friend, to the BrathelLanza."

I didn't know what he was talking about, or much care right at the moment, and let whatever consciousness I had left slip away from me.

2

A Visiting Shadow

I have only vague recollections of the next half hour or so, though I dimly recall being half dragged, half carried into the building to which RyoNa had led me, and down a long, dimly lighted corridor to the doors of what must have been a huge cargo elevator—at the time I could only vaguely wonder at the presence of the elevator in a decaying building in the city's worst slums. The elevator doors closed behind us, I seem to remember, and then there was the sensation of dropping, going down, down, down. And that's all I can remember for a while.

When I opened my eyes next I was lying on a cot in a small room illuminated by a single strip of light that ran across the ceiling, a dim light that revealed damp walls of concrete or stone. To my nostrils came the odors of stagnation and decay, as if this room had been long unused, and when it was used it wasn't for the most pleasant of purposes.

RyoNa stood not far from the cot on which I lay, a vague smile on his face. Behind him stood two of the black-clad apes, one on each side of the doorway, and they looked at me without kindness or sympathy. I thought that the big red bruise on the cheek of one of them might have something to do with their lack of friendliness.

At last RyoNa spoke, and the tone of his voice was more friendly than the looks I was getting from his companions. "It's unfortunate that it had to be this way, Harkos." HarkosNor was the name by which RyoNa knew me. "But I could hardly be certain of

13

your cooperation once—well, once you found out that I really have no connections with the chronal-displacement project at all."

I suppose I should have been surprised, and if my head hadn't hurt so much I might have been, but right then I was only disappointed. He'd lied to me, strung me along—not that such a thing seemed greatly out of character for him—but to what end I couldn't then guess. As I was about to open my mouth and try to get my voice working so that I could ask him, he spoke again.

"Others will be coming soon to speak with you, some very important people, and they will answer your questions for you, so don't even ask them of me. I was instructed to say that you are valued highly and that they would prefer that you suffer no more hurt."

"I'd prefer it that way myself," I finally managed to say.

"I'm sure," RyoNa said, then took a hesitant step forward and fished something out of the folds of his dark robe. "This may be of some help to you." He bent forward, still more than an arm's reach from the cot where I lay, and placed a small bottle on the floor. "Drink that. It won't hurt you and may help to relieve the pain in your head."

I looked at the bottle with suspicion and then back at RyoNa with the same feeling.

"If we wanted you dead, you would already be dead," he said, with the hint of a smile on his lips. "And why should we waste time with poison?"

Maybe he had a point there.

Then he backed to the doorway and allowed one of the black-clad characters to open the door for him. As he disappeared between them, he said, "Please wait as patiently as you can, Harkos. The others should be here soon."

The two men in black, still looking uglily at me, moved through the doorway and closed the door behind them. I heard the distinct sound of a heavy bolt sliding home. _Clack!_ Sure, I'd wait. What else could I do?

I lay still for a while before I carefully lifted myself from the cot and went to get the little bottle of color-less liquid that RyoNa had left for me. Maybe it was something to help my head; with the passage of time the pain in it had not lessened much. It could have been something other than what he'd claimed, but, on the probability that it was a painkiller, I decided to take it. What did I have to lose now anyway?

The simple movement from the cot to the bottle and back again was enough to double the pounding in my head and make me wonder if the blow had caused a concussion, or worse. I drank the liquid—right then I might have taken it even if I'd strongly suspected it to be something worse than it actually was.

There was an oily, fruity taste to it and the tang of alcohol, and it burned my throat as it went down, but almost instantly I began to feel better, or thought I did.

In a few minutes I could sit up on the side of the cot, feeling something not greatly worse than a moder-ate hangover, and that too seemed to be passing. I silently thanked RyoNa for the medicine, if for nothing else.

With the passing of the pain I was able to examine my new surroundings a little more closely, though I found them of little interest. The cot was the room's only article of furniture. Three of the walls were flat, damp concrete, I saw now, with a slightly slimy feel when I touched them with my fingertips. The fourth wall was different only in that a door had been cut in it, a heavy door that seemed to have been made from a single piece of wood, which I knew to be bolted from the outside. The floor was made of the same concrete as the walls, and so was the ceiling, which was distinguished only by the dimly glowing strip that ran from one of the side walls to the other. From inside the room there appeared no means either of turning off the light or of controlling its intensity. And exactly how the strip, which appeared to be made of translucent plastic maybe a quarter of an inch thick and three inches wide, produced its light, I didn't know, nor did I concern myself greatly with it.

Having examined the room and discovered nothing that would help me out of my predicament, I went back to the cot, sat down, and was about to begin what I hoped to be a dispassionate analysis of my situation, when I became aware of something else in the room, something that had not been there a moment before.

In one of the two corners most remote from the door, in the shadows where the glowing strip illuminated to an even lesser extent, there seemed to be the beginning of the formation of a cloud of smoke, hazy wisps turning slowly in the air, extending from the floor nearly to the ceiling. There was also, in the atmosphere, even less tangible but nonetheless real, a sensation that had become an almost familiar one to me: a sense of electrical tension, a feeling such as one sometimes has at the approach of a thunderstorm, the sense of power that you can't see or hear or touch or smell but that you know is there.

The smokiness in the corner grew thicker, more intense, more opaque, and now had begun to take on the shape I'd come to expect—from top to bottom the hazy form was about the height of a man, and, like a man, it had the outlines of two legs, a torso, two arms, a head set above shadowy shoulders, though within the head there could be discerned no facial features whatsoever. Now the shadow, the haze, had solidified as far as I thought it would, had become as substantial as it could.

I waited for the Shadowy Man to speak, as I knew he would.

"Well, Eric," the voice said out of the haze, a voice uncertain at first, then more positive, a voice that I knew to sound exactly like my own, "I hope you're not feeling too badly now."

I shook my head. "I'm okay." Then I said to him, "I was afraid the Tromas had destroyed you back in KHL-000." He knew what I was talking about.

A chuckle came out of the shadowy haze. "Damn," my voice said from the corner, "this could get confusing."

"What do you mean?" I asked.

"What you're talking about is in your past, you see," the Shadowy Man said, "but it's in *my* future. It hasn't happened to *me* yet, so I don't know the outcome of our fight with the Krithian ladies any more than you do."

"I see," I said, though I wasn't certain that I did.

"I hope you do, though I'm not positive I do. As I said, it *could* get confusing."

"Yeah," I said, and grunted, and then waited for him to tell me whatever it was he had to tell me. He'd come for a reason, I was certain of that.

"Your head's not hurting now, and don't worry, you don't have a concussion. That lump will go away in a few days."

"That's comforting," I said, despite myself feeling awe in *his* presence, and still wondering just what our relationship was/would be, for somehow in the confusion of time future and time past, the Shadowy Man and I were very closely linked, terribly closely.

"And I suggest that the best thing for you will be to cooperate with the members of the BrathelLanza when they come to visit you."

"The what?" That word again!

"The BrathelLanza," he repeated. "You'll find out what it is in due time. For now, cooperate with them as fully as possible, for from cooperating with them will come answers to the questions you want to ask of me, and a means of action."

"A means of action?" I asked stupidly.

"Yes, a means of action, the action that will bring . . . well, you'll see," he said, and chuckled as if he were playing a very funny joke on me.

"What in—" I started to ask, but it was already too late. The haziness in the corner was beginning to lose its manlike form, to become vague, mixing fogs that dissipated even more quickly than they had formed. The electrical tension was gone from the air.

"Damn!" I said aloud, and got up from the cot and walked to the corner. There was nothing there, of course. Nothing at all.

"Why do you have to be so damned mysterious?" I asked the empty air, and if I did hear a chuckle for answer, I was probably imagining it. Wasn't I?

I sat back down on the cot, cursed the Shadowy Man—whoever, whatever, he was—wished for a cigarette, of which I had none, or a cup of coffee, of which I had as little, and wondered just exactly what it was this "BrathelLanza" had in store for me. Probably not a time machine—not if RyoNa had finally been telling me the truth. Then what? Answers? "A means of action." Now what did that mean?

Damn, damn, damn, I said to myself, and sat on the edge of the cot and waited for the arrival of those "very important people" that RyoNa had promised were coming.

3

From the Far World to VarKhohs

While I waited in that dim, dank cell somewhere under the city of VarKhohs on a Timeline that the beings I called Kriths had been very secretive about—though not secretive enough, it seemed at the time—I found that despite myself I was reviewing the events of the past year or so, the sequence of events that had led me from what had been a rather comfortable if sometimes dangerous condition to one far less comfortable and perhaps even more dangerous, and I wondered about the wisdom of some of the decisions I'd made; even up until three or four months ago I could have stayed out of it—I think—and lived not a bad life with Sally way off there on a world of the far Temporal-East. But my curiosity, and maybe a taste for vengeance, wouldn't let me . . . and here I was.

Thanks to the help of this mysterious Shadowy Man —whoever, whatever he is—Sally and I had escaped from the Tromas on KHL-000, had escaped to a place the Shadowy Man had picked out for us, a pleasant enough world a long way to the T-East where we probably could have spent the rest of our lives in comfort, if I hadn't been so damned stubborn, so damned curious, so damned determined to see if I could get in a lick against the Kriths.

The Shadowy Man had provided us with a skudder and I couldn't resist, sooner or later, using it. Somewhere, somewhen in time, I was to be mixed up with the Shadowy Man again, was somehow to become a part of him, it seemed, and to do that I was going to have to be able to move about in time itself, future time and past time. I had to have a time machine. So I thought.

Once I was certain that Sally would have no problems if I were gone, would live like a queen or a demi-goddess in the semibarbaric kingdoms of the world we'd found, I went back to the skudder in the woods, leaving her a note that told her what I was doing and why. I hoped she'd understand. And I was going to miss her like crazy, but I couldn't let her risk her life again by going along with my insane ideas. *Maybe* I'd be able to come back to her.

So, like that thief in the night, I took the skudder the Shadowy Man had provided for us, and set off across the Lines to see what I could find.

Specifically what I was looking for was the one known world that had developed/would develop a device capable of moving about in time. I was relatively certain that such a world did exist, although finding it wasn't easy.

Like the spectrum of a beam of sunlight shown on paper through a prism, there is no sharp distinction from world to world, but only very subtle changes that over a vast number of parallel worlds can lead to surprising differences. World B might differ from world A only in something so minor as the first name of a head of state in a rather unimportant nation. In world C that same head of state might have a different last name, and in world D he might have a somewhat different personality that would give his nation a chance for success in a minor war that it wouldn't have had in worlds A and B. By the time you get to world J, that nation might not be so minor and on world Z it might dominate the planet. Or destroy it.

So I had to search large areas of paratime, moving carefully from world to world, searching for clues that would tell me I was at least heading in the right direction.

And on one world where I spent more than a few days, a world with a more highly developed medical science than most, I found a not-too-scrupulous surgeon who removed the transmitter the Kriths had buried in my body long before. I gave the surgeon a large amount of gold and he gave me a local anesthetic, and while I watched, my hand resting on the butt of my energy pistol, he removed and destroyed the telltale. I thanked him and went on my way, hopeful that Kriths wouldn't find me as easily as they had before, if they were still looking for me. And I suspected they were.

At last, by following leads and hints and rumors too obscure to go into now, I found the world for which I had been searching, or at least I thought I had found it. I hoped I had.

I skudded into that particular world when it was late at night in eastern North America and hid my skudder near a small town not too distant from what appeared to be the major city of the continent, Var-Khohs, capital of NakrehVatee. The language here, called EKhona, was a remote kin of one I'd learned on another Line when in the service of the Kriths, so fortunately it didn't take me too long to master the local speech. It took me a little longer to get the hang of local customs, but I managed to stay out of jail and trade some of the large quantity of finely worked gold I'd brought along for local currency. With that I was able to buy myself a computer identity that would account for my light skin, my accent, and my relative ignorance of the ways of the world: I was a mercenary soldier named HarkosNor from the Central European country of SteeMehseeh, who had bought his way out of indenture with loot gained in a brush-fire war in the Far East and who had applied for a visa to enter NakrehVatee, where he would seek permission to join the nation's "foreign legion" and serve again as a mercenary. The man who sold me the identity, a shady type who I hoped was more trust-worthy than he looked, assured me that HarkosNor was a real person, though dead now, and that my identity would hold up under the closest scrutiny. I hoped he wasn't lying.

So there I was, officially, if illegally, a member of the local culture. I was as as ready as I'd ever be to go into the city of VarKhohs to try to find myself a time machine.

Finding what I was searching for was just about as difficult as finding this world in the first place, but there are always people around who are ready to offer information about supposedly secret things if you cross their palms in the proper fashion. Thus it was that after several weeks in VarKhohs I began spending a great deal of time in a place with an unpronounce-able name that was a combination restaurant, lounge, massage parlor, steam bath, and brothel, frequented by members of a moderately-high caste and their hangers-on—the caste given over to electronic engineering and other technologies. And it was there that I made the acquaintance of a certain RyoNa, not a technician himself, but a member of one of the administrative castes and supposedly a friend of the engineers and technicians.

It would have been difficult to say exactly what time it was, getting on toward the wee hours, and both my new friend RyoNa and I were close to exhaustion. We'd eaten and drunk our fill in the lower levels of the elaborate and luxurious pleasure-house and then had moved upward to the levels devoted to the games and the girls. We'd gambled for a while, losing more than we won, and had picked up a brace of twins, girls even darker of skin than most of the locals, with long black hair and flashing black eyes, dressed in styles that revealed not only their profession but the lovely tools of their trade. As they led us off to their bedroom apartments in the towering building, I felt a pang of guilt at betraying Sally, again, and wondered if she was being as faithful to me as I was to her. I hoped not!

We parted company, RyoNa and his girl, I and mine, and indulged ourselves in the wicked pleasures of the flesh—and I discovered that the dark-skinned girl, whose name I'd already forgotten, was a past mistress of the arts of sexual pleasure. When I'd finally told her good-bye, with a kiss and a handful of bank notes, I was totally exhausted and felt the beginnings of a hangover.

Downstairs, in one of the lounges, I found my buddy RyoNa exactly where he'd said he would be, drinking a dark, heavy liquid from a tall tumbler. A similar tumbler, this one full, was on the opposite side of the table.

"Sit down, Harkos," RyoNa said, seemingly still amused by the outlandishness of my name. "I've already ordered for you."

"I see. What is it?" I asked as I sat down.

"Try it."

I did, and found it to be a very pleasant fruit mixture that probably would have been rated ninety proof or better on a world that rated alcoholic content in that fashion.

"Is it good?" RyoNa asked.

I grunted, nodded.

"And was she good?"

I grunted, nodded again.

"I told you she would be. Those EstarSimirian girls are just about the best around. Raised from childhood to master the arts of bed pleasure, you know."

"I certainly wasn't disappointed," I told him with a weary sigh.

"And what did she think of you?"

"Me?"

RyoNa nodded, and smiled with a wicked gleam

in his eyes. "It is very rare for a fair-skinned barbarian to bed with the girls of a VarKhohs pleasure-house."

"Oh, yeah." I sighed, and sipped my drink again.

Though I hadn't yet really begun to sort out the history of this world and its many cultures, I had some idea of what he was referring to. The fair-skinned people of northern Europe, on this Line, were not the first ones to develop a technological civilization. That fell to the darker people of the eastern Mediterranean, western Asia, and northern Africa. It was they who first sailed the "Inland Sea" and learned to tack against the wind and who finally set out into the great oceans of the West and of the Southeast, who circumnavigated the globe for the first time and then began to colonize the New World, who built steam engines and invented things like the telegraph and telephone and the airplane, and who ignited the first atomic bomb somewhere in Africa and burned away the better part of a great city.

The blue-eyed blonds, of which I am one even though as a child I spoke a version of Greek, had been to the Asians as the American Indians had been to the Europeans who colonized North America in Sally's world: savages to be dispossessed of their land for the benefit of the "more civilized" people from the South and the East. Long years of warfare followed, during which most of the natives of northern Europe were exterminated, though when the wars came to an end, the surviving Europeans, by then hardened by decades of combat, came to be a warrior caste among the spreading colonists, a people apart, to be used to wage their wars.

Such a one to them I seemed, accepted now as nearly an equal by the "enlightened moderns," but still—was I feared, or respected, or looked upon with a kind of awe by people to whom active participation in warfare was a thing of the past?

"I don't suppose I greatly disappointed her," I said at last, finishing my drink.

"Another," RyoNa said, a statement, not a question, and punched out another set of drinks on the table's ordering keys. "I doubt you did disappoint her. By Themfo-Okketho, what a pair you two must have been! I wish I could have watched."

"I'm exhausted," I said.

"No doubt the girl is too."

"She may be."

"Oh, when I go to my tomb and journey to the Dark Lands, I'd like to take an EstarSimirian whore with me, the Dark Lords willing."

When the drinks came, delivered by a waitress of low caste, clad as revealingly as the dark girls had been, RyoNa was silent for a while, then cast his eyes about the darkened room in a conspiratorial manner.

"I will name no names, friend Harkos," he said, "nor state any facts. But I believe I know where to find the man you seek."

"The man I seek? What do you mean?"

"No names. No facts. But you have let slip to me that there is a certain *thing* you would like to have access to. Is this not so?"

"Yes, there is a thing I need."

"A thing the very existence of which is supposed to be known to only a few, is this not so?"

I nodded. We were talking about a prototype of one of the chronal-displacement devices, and we both knew it. My hints in the past had been sufficient to establish that.

"It is one of the earlier models, you know," he said softly. "Not as refined as the ones now being tested, but it seems to do the job for which it was designed."

"Where is it?"

"Ah." He sighed. "That I cannot say. But let me say this: it is not where it is supposed to be. It was to be sent to one of the nations allied to NakrehVatee, a nation whose name I cannot speak. It was shipped, but it never arrived at its destination. A—shall we say, a friend of mine knows its present location."

"Can you take me to this friend?" I asked.

"It may be possible. I must visit him myself and discuss with him the arrangements. It will be very costly."

"I had anticipated that."

"*Very* costly."

"How much?"

He stated a figure that would be meaningless without a knowledge of the local currency, but it was a high one, one that I thought I could just barely meet. I'd brought a lot of gold with me.

"Very well," RyoNa said, once I'd nodded in agreement. "When I go to visit my friend I will need a token of your good faith."

"How much?"

"Ten per cent should suffice."

"When?"

"The day after tomorrow, mid-afternoon. Meet me here. It must be in hard currency. No paper."

"It will be."

"Very good."

We finished our drinks in silence and then departed the pleasure-house.

At the appointed time I sat in the pleasure-house lounge with a sack that held the hard currency, small, flat bars of platinum embossed with the symbols of the highest castes of VarKhohs. I had just finished my drink when RyoNa entered, took a seat across from me, and waited while I ordered drinks for us.

"You have it?"

I passed the leather sack to him under the table. I felt like a fool. What did I know of this RyoNa? How far could I trust him?

"Good," he said. "I will drink my drink and then

I must go. Wait here for me. I should be back shortly before dark. I will then have the arrangements."

"Okay." I sighed, and sipped my fresh drink, while he swallowed his in a single gulp and then rose and left the lounge.

After a short wait I rose to follow him. He probably expected me to.

Damned right he'd expected me to!

That's how I'd ended up in a cell, remembering all this while I waited for his "very important people" to visit me.

4

Into the Underground

It wouldn't be correct to say that the time was inter-
minable, but it was much longer than I would have
liked, alone in the cramped room under the earth, but
at last RyoNa did return and with him were three
others, as well as the two black-clad guards, who
may have been outside the room the whole time.

The guards entered the room first, looked me over
carefully as if there were some means by which I could
have gained weapons in their absence—fat chance!—
and then stood on either side of the open door. RyoNa
entered next and suggested I get up off the cot and
remain standing. Remembering what the Shadowy Man
had said, I stood up.

AkweNema, so the first man was introduced, a name
that had an almost familiar ring to it, though I couldn't
recall where I'd heard it. He was a big man, larger
and heavier even than RyoNa, more given to fat, with
long hair of an unexpected, astonishing red and a
florid cast to his swarthy complexion. This North
America too was a melting pot of racial types, it
seemed. His robes were rich and dazzling, of a dark
red material with silvery piping that reflected the
room's dim light, and he wore the symbols of an
elevated caste and of the medical profession on his
chest and sparkling rings on his fingers.

AkweNema bowed slightly when introduced, a gesture he expected me to reproduce, which I did, and
then he looked me over with an intelligent if somewhat
piercing gaze, and with a bit of the clinical about it.

28

I later learned that he was, in fact, a medical doctor, among other things.

Then he nodded to RyoNa and gave him a pleasant, you-have-done-well sort of smile. RyoNa was pleased and I felt like a side of beef that he had just procured for AkweNema's pantry.

The second man was smaller than either AkweNema or RyoNa, a slender, almost wizened man of indeterminate age, with bright eyes set deep in their sockets under heavy eyebrows. He could have been fifty years old or he could have been seventy. He too was dressed in the luxurious robes of one of the higher castes, a technologically oriented one, I suspected from the decoration of his robe, and if I read the symbols rightly, he practiced his profession in the academic manner of a university instructor. His name was Kaph-No and he carried an honorific that could just barely be translated as "professor."

The third man was the youngest, in his late twenties, I suspected, although his full beard initially gave the impression of someone older, as did his eyes and the premature streak of gray in his long, carefully coiffured hair. Though his robes were less lavish than those of the first two, the symbols on his chest were those of one of the highest castes of all. Lord Dessa-Tyso, as he was named, stood closer to the peak of the social pyramid than did the others, although I soon began to suspect that he was in a lesser position to exercise actual power than were his two older companions. He affected a bored, supercilious expression and I thought that he had probably been very spoiled as a child.

That he was still spoiled, I learned later.

When the introductions were completed and the three men had finished their inspections of me, Akwe-Nema, the headman and ringleader, spoke again. "We have no desire to constrain you against your will, Master HarkosNor"—he addressed me as a gentleman of his own social rank: odd—"though we will do so if necessary. We would prefer your cooperation, and I suspect that once you know who we are and what we are doing, and once you have seen the rewards we have to offer you"—he paused in mid-sentence and smiled—"and once you have forgiven us for the deception we played on you, we think you will be very willing to cooperate."

I was already, I thought, but I'd want to know more very soon. Addressing him as an equal, I said, "Master AkweNema, this hasn't been a very pleasant welcome you've given me, and I'd like to know what you're up to. Right now all I can feel is cheated and used."

"Very shortly we will explain it all to you, I promise," AkweNema replied in a conciliatory tone. "If you will give us your word, for the time being, that you will attempt neither to escape nor to use violence against any of us, we will allow you a certain limited freedom under your own recognizance."

"For how long?" I asked.

"Until you have let us speak our piece and we have made you an offer," the big, red-haired man said.

"And if I refuse your offer?"

"I doubt that you will," he said.

"We shall speak of that later, Master HarkosNor," said the lord DessaTyso, using the condescending address of a superior to his social inferior.

"Come," AkweNema said in a jovial tone of voice, "I am certain that this place is as unpleasant to you as it is to us. Let us go to a place where we can relax and have a cup of wine."

I shrugged.

"Then you will give us your word?" the lord DessaTyso asked.

"Yeah," I said, and grunted, giving his rank no recognition. "What have I got to lose?"

Lord DessaTyso gave me a crooked smile but didn't speak.

"RyoNa, you may go," AkweNema said. "We will contact you when we need you."

"Very good, sir," RyoNa said, using the address one would use to a social superior, though not quite as honorable an address as the one he might have used toward the lord DessaTyso. Then he turned to face me. "You'll think better of me when these gentlemen have had their say, Harkos."

I just looked at him without speaking.

With a shrug toward me and a bow toward the others, he turned and left, and as he did I thought I could hear the jingle of platinum bars in a leather sack he carried under his robe. A good day's pay for services rendered.

"You are excused as well," AkweNema said to the guards at the door, who gave me unfriendly looks as they left the room. They seemed not to think as highly of me as AkweNema did. "And now, gentlemen and sire, to my suite, if you will."

AkweNema led us from the room, with Professor KaphNo directly behind him. Lord DessaTyso was careful to stay at my side. I wondered if he was armed. I suspected so.

The first part of the journey was through what must have been some very old underground service tunnels, no longer in use, saved from total decay by the efforts of AkweNema's people. The tunnels had been cleaned up and buttressed to prevent their collapse and had been provided with illumination strips sufficient for safe passage through the tunnels. But this wasn't where the bulk of their efforts had been exerted.

We had gone perhaps half a mile through the underground passages when we came to a metal wall that blocked the tunnel from floor to ceiling, and through which passed a pair of heavy metal doors, which were guarded by two burly, black-clad men carrying automatic pistols and with what might have been gas grenades clipped to their belts.

AkweNema spoke a greeting to them, to which they responded by opening the doors, allowing us to pass into another section of the Underground. The guards eyed me with suspicion, but, unlike their fellows, not with open hatred. They hadn't been among the bunch on the surface.

Once we were through the metal doorway I saw that here a great deal more than simple cleaning and bracing of the tunnel walls had been done. Bright parallel strips of illumination, like glowing railroad tracks, dwindled in the distance of the long, long corridors. The walls had been smoothed and painted or paneled and were decorated with bright photographs of outdoor scenes of the world above and with vividly graphic posters that said such things as THE WORLD IS AWAITING OUR COMING and THE FUTURE RESTS IN THE HANDS OF THE BRATHELLANZA and THE CHILDREN OF TOMORROW WILL BE OURS. Carpeting had been laid across the floor, soft and cushiony. Doors led off from the tunnel into other chambers cut into the earth and stone. Far ahead I could hear voices and the movement of men and machinery.

Just inside the metal doorway an attractive young woman in a bright blue gown sat behind a desk, and to each of us she handed a yellow disk, which we fixed to the fronts of our robes. AkweNema, making no introductions, asked her, "Is my suite ready?"

The girl smiled, nodded, and said, "Yes, sir, it is."

"Please have food and drink delivered there. We are not to be disturbed until you are notified."

"Yes, sir," the girl said again. "But, ah, sir, the lady OrDjina has been asking about his lordship."

DessaTyso shot a quick glance at AkweNema, who nodded in return. "I don't suppose her being there would create any problem." To the girl: "Inform Lady OrDjina that she is more than welcome."

"Very good, sir."

And with that AkweNema led us on again, a hundred yards or so down the brightly lighted tunnel, to a large wooden door before which stood an elderly man in a simple blue uniform. Without speaking, the man bowed and opened the door for AkweNema.

"Food is coming," AkweNema said to the blue-clad servant. "Please see to it."

"Very good, sire." The servant used a higher form of address than had the girl at the desk; he hung from lower rungs of the social ladder.

The lord DessaTyso and I followed AkweNema and KaphNo through the doorway.

A series of lavish rooms lay beyond the wooden door, though at first I saw only one of them, the first and largest, something that could almost have been out of *The Arabian Nights:* plush carpets and great down-filled cushions in place of chairs; tables on which sat beautifully detailed vases and tall, elaborate lamps; wall hangings and tapestries of the richest materials, the most complex of designs (made by hand or by computer-directed looms? I wondered); in the middle of the room stood a marble sculpture of a mermaid rising from the sea; in the background, a beautiful if esoteric music played.

"Sit down, gentlemen and my lord. Refreshments should be arriving soon," AkweNema said. "I trust that you could do with food and drink, Master Harkos-Nor."

"I could," I admitted.

As we sat down on the cushions, again DessaTyso looked me over carefully, coldly, as if inspecting a horse someone had offered to sell him—or a slave. I didn't care much for his appraisal and I tried to tell him so with a cold, hard look of my own. He must have caught my meaning, for he smiled crookedly and looked away without speaking.

"We must wait a bit more, HarkosNor," AkweNema said. "It would be inhospitable on my part to begin our talk without offering you refreshment."

I nodded and continued to look around the room, trying to estimate, in terms of some monetary system, the cost of the items that filled the apartment. A fortune, easily, but exactly how great a fortune I couldn't guess.

The lord DessaTyso appeared to be on the verge of speaking when there came a rap on the door, gentle, servile, but clearly audible, and then the door opened to allow the blue-clad steward to enter, pushing a great wheeled cart that looked too big for him, and which was laden with bottles and goblets and dishes and covered bowls. As he entered and was about to close the door behind him, another person appeared and was framed for a moment in the open doorway.

"OrDjina," DessaTyso called out, half rising to his feet and gesturing for the newcomer to enter. "Please come in."

"Yes, please do, my lady," AkweNema said, also rising halfway and getting off an awkward little bow.

I figured I might as well rise too, as the others had done.

Old KaphNo, silent and perhaps brooding, made no effort to rise.

The woman, who brushed around the steward and came into the room, was almost enough to make me catch my breath in my throat. To say that she was beautiful is hardly adequate.

Perhaps in her early thirties, mature and fully in possession of herself, she was tall, nearly six feet I would have guessed, and beautifully proportioned. She wore a dark, clinging gown that molded itself to the contours of her body, revealing and yet hiding each line and curve of her torso and legs; her arms were bare except for silvery bracelets on her forearms and dazzling rings on her fingers.

She had dark, dusky skin the color of an old and highly polished piece of prized oak, and long black hair that trailed down her back to below her shoulder blades; tiny gems, like stars, twinkled in her hair. Her eyes were large, black, bright, intelligent; her lips, very full, covered perfect, bright white teeth that showed as she now smiled at us, as she entered the room and closed the door behind her.

It was only later that I realized that there were no badges of rank and caste on her breast, and wondered why.

"Thank you, AkweNema," she said, equal-to-equal, briefly offering the man her hand. Her voice was melodious and rich, a slightly husky alto. She could have had a great career as a singer or an actress, I thought.

She nodded to KaphNo and spoke his name, but she seemed to expect no reply other than the upward glance that came from under his bushy eyebrows. Then her gaze came to me.

"And you must be the barbarian warrior Harkos-Nor," she said, offering her hand, which I briefly clasped as AkweNema had done. I could detect no condescension in her voice.

"I am HarkosNor," I replied.

When she had retrieved her hand, perhaps pleased that all the fingers were still there, she went on past me to where the lord DessaTyso again sat on the cushioned floor, there to sit down beside him and take one of his hands fondly between both of hers.

Yes, I told myself, the lord DessaTyso is still very much the spoiled princeling.

By this time the steward thought it safe to move again, and rolled the food-and-wine-laden cart into the middle of the room, up next to the mermaid sculpture.

"Shall I serve you now, sire?" he asked of Akwe-Nema in a servile tone of voice.

"No, no," AkweNema said, dismissing him with a wave of his fat hand. "We can serve ourselves. You may go."

"Thank you, sire." The blue-clad man then quietly vanished.

"Then let us eat," AkweNema said, rising again and crossing to the cart the steward had brought in. "Then we may talk."

While we ate, and while I glanced in OrDjina's direction whenever the conversation would decently allow—a conversation of small talk that I could barely follow, talk of palace intrigues among the higher castes of VarKhohs, of hinted scandals, of corrupted bureaucracy burdened almost to the point of self-destruction by its own complexities—I wondered just what it was that AkweNema and his friends would have to say when the time for serious talk finally arrived.

And I remembered again the Shadowy Man's most recent advice. His advice had served me well in the past, though some of the things he had led me into hadn't always been of the most pleasant nature.

How would this one turn out? I wondered.

5
The BrathelLanza's Proposal

"Master HarkosNor," AkweNema began over tall goblets of white wine after the meal was finished, a "snack," he had said, which had consisted of several courses of fish and fowl and flesh, "we know that you are a stranger in our land and have been among our people for only a short while, and we know that you have come here in the hope of gaining for yourself one of the so-called time machines that our technicians supposedly have built and are testing."

"Chronal-displacement devices," KaphNo threw in, his voice a bitter grumbling. I think it was the first time he'd spoken since we'd arrived in AkweNema's suite.

"I stand corrected," AkweNema said, smiling. "Chronal-displacement devices." The smile went away. "And for what purpose you wish one we do not know. It is no concern of ours." His face said differently; and I wondered what he thought a barbarian warrior like HarkosNor wanted with a time machine—to go back into time to save his people from the humiliation of subjugation, or merely to get away to a simpler world where a warrior stood in higher honor? "But we may be able to help you get one, since that is your wish," he was saying.

"I thought that was what RyoNa was in the process of doing earlier today," I said, letting my voice sound as bitter and angry as I dared.

"I can understand your feelings," AkweNema said, "and I understand your anger at us. Your anger may seem justified to you now, but please hold it in abey-

37

ance for a while." He paused, sighed, then continued: "I am afraid that RyoNa lied to you in several respects. There is no time—no chronal-displacement device in all of NakrehVatee, nor in all the world, that is not under the heaviest of guard. There are, in fact, only four of them in existence, and they do not work nearly as well as the popular imagination would lead you to believe, and may never—and, in addition, it would be impossible for you to gain one of them, imperfect as they are, without the aid of an army, or without the aid of a new government in power in NakrehVatee."

I gave him back stare for stare but didn't speak.

"Which brings me to my point," he said. "With *your* aid, we can provide you with both—an army *and* a new government.

"As a newcomer to our land, you may be ignorant of the many injustices that now exist in our nation. We may be the greatest power on Earth today, but as things stand now our society is rotten to the core. Over the years the caste system, which has many good and truly admirable points, has been abused by certain groups in positions of power. The castes themselves have multiplied and subdivided to such an extent that the whole system has become unwieldy and at times even self-destructive.

"New castes have been formed as offshoots of older castes to serve new functions as society has developed, which is well and good; but older castes whose functions have ceased to be of value continue to exist, and those born into them, some of the lower ones, have no way out of them, save through death and hopefully a better change during their next reincarnation, if they as individuals have earned the karma for another chance at life."

The eyes of the others in the room were more on me than on AkweNema. I hoped my face looked as noncommittal as I was trying to make it look.

"We have, on the one extreme," AkweNema was saying, "castes in positions of power and wealth that have no useful function and are only parasitic to society, consuming vast quantities of goods and services, yet contributing nothing. And on the other extreme are castes which have fallen far down the scale of society and now exist to no good purpose, consuming little, but with their members doomed to live in poverty and hunger, with no hope of ever finding gainful employment in their present lives. They are sustained only by thoughts of the Dark Lords and passage beyond the lands over which they rule, for what need is there for a caste of chimney sweeps when there are no chimneys left to sweep? Castes such as those are also parasitic to society, though I'm certain that the people who are members of them do not wish to be.

"Let me say here, Master HarkosNor, that we of the BrathelLanza—the Brotherhood of Life—are not anarchists or wild-eyed radicals out to destroy the caste system entirely. Not at all. We merely wish to purify it, to restore it to the state of cleanliness that made NakrehVatee the great nation it once was not so many years ago."

KaphNo looked up briefly, a crooked, unpleasant smile on his face as if he had just bitten into a lemon and didn't want to admit how sour it was.

"Our goal," AkweNema said, "is to return a better life to the castes, to the people, of our nation."

As he talked further of the evils he saw in the present society of NakrehVatee, as he further enumerated the wrongs that must be put right and how the BrathelLanza would go about doing it, his words came more quickly, more harshly, and there came into his eyes a gleam I didn't like, a glow perhaps of fanaticism, or of madness.

And when I glanced at the other faces, I saw reflected in their eyes that gleam I'd seen in AkweNema's.

I'd gotten myself mixed up with a bunch of fanatical revolutionaries, by God!

But the Shadowy Man had said . . .

It may have been thirty minutes later when Akwe-Nema finally came to find a specific direction in his harangue.

"So we have banded together in the BrathelLanza," he said, "the Brotherhood of Life that will set things right in NakrehVatee, Lord DessaTyso and Professor KaphNo and myself, Ladies OrDjina and EnDera, Drs. ThefeRa and SkorTho, psychologist GrelLo, and the many others whom you will meet in the coming days, if you agree to join us in our sacred cause.

"We have formed cadres all over the nation, and the people who believe as we do, who believe that the time has come to cleanse the nation, have come to us, have joined us. We are training them and arming them so that when the day comes we can rise as one force, solidified in our resolve and our commitment, and put down those in positions of ill-gained power."

He paused, licked his dry lips. I wondered how much of his speech had been memorized and how much of it had come to him as he spoke.

"We have already formed the nucleus of the new government," AkweNema continued, his voice calmer now. "Lord DessaTyso will be our chief of state, for such has been his training from birth and such is the right his lordship has inherited from his magnificent ancestors, the founders of our state." Lord DessaTyso smiled broadly and basked in OrDjina's obvious admiration. "With humility, KaphNo and I will do our best to serve as his ministers Sinister and Dexter. The cabinet largely has been appointed and will join us here when the time comes. The people will supply the new parliament when the castes have been purged."

"And when will all this take place?" I asked when he paused again.

"We will rise a year from now, perhaps," Akwe-Nema said. "I hope no longer in time than that. You, Master HarkosNor, can be a factor in helping us determine the date."

"Okay," I said. "So you've got a place somewhere for me in all this. But where it is I can't imagine."

"We need a fighting man to lead our troops," Akwe-Nema said, "and we need the nucleus of a fighting force that we hope to make superior to anything the government presently has in the field."

"And I can do that?" I asked incredulously.

"We believe you can," he replied. "We have studied you from the day you first approached our agent RyoNa," he admitted. "For example, the girls you have slept with—they are all our people, and they have studied you well."

"Oh?" I said.

He nodded. "We have also checked your background, and we find it of the sort we need. Your experience in combat is greater than that of any other man your age in all of VarKhohs, perhaps all of NakrehVatee," AkweNema told me.

And I thought: The guy who sold me my computer identity said it would be everything I'd ever need. I guess he was right. It had cost enough.

"We are satisfied with you, HarkosNor," DessaTyso said. "You are the sort of man we need."

"Then will you join us?" AkweNema asked.

"What exactly do you want of me?" I asked in reply.

"You shall be our general in the field. You and your private army"—he smiled as he said these words—"will spearhead the takeover of the central government buildings of VarKhohs."

Old KaphNo looked up from under his eyebrows. "You are familiar with the concept of cloning, are you not, Master HarkosNor?"

"Of course," I said, wondering why he asked.

And as if I hadn't answered, he continued: "Every

cell of the human body—save only the sex cells designed for diversity in the next generation and a few very specialized cells like those of the blood—holds a complete genetic blueprint of the parent body. That is, every bit of genetic information that existed at the time of your conception, in the combined sperm and egg of your parents that grew to be you in your mother's womb, is repeated in exact replication in the cells of, say, the skin of your left index finger, or in the cells of your intestinal lining."

I nodded, beginning to suspect. Sometimes I may be slow, but I'm not *that* dense.

"From any one of those cells," old KaphNo went on, "under the proper conditions, there can be grown an exact duplicate of you, HarkosNor, down to the last detail." He paused, then added: "Except, of course, for the effects that environment has had on you. A clone grown from the cells of HarkosNor would have neither the scars you carry on your body nor the memories you carry in your head."

I nodded, then said, "I know."

"We propose, then," AkweNema picked up after KaphNo grew silent, "to take sample cells from your body—a simple and painless operation, I assure you—and from them *grow* an army of your physical duplicates, an army which you will train and which you will command."

"There is a phenomenon called 'resonance,'" KaphNo said. "Through it, so it appears, the senior member of a replicated partnership or group—in this case, yourself—is able to exercise a significant degree of, shall we say, telepathic control over the junior members. It is not yet well understood, although the same or a similar phenomenon—'sympathetic awareness,' it is often called—was long ago first observed in identical twins, which have many similarities to multiple replicates.

"Furthermore, resonance is even more pronounced when the senior of a replicated unit is an adult at the time of replication. During the later stages of maturation, so it seems, the senior may totally dominate the 'offspring' replicates: that is, by moving in before the brains of the replicates have been exposed to any significant number of external stimuli—we'll go into more detail regarding all this later—and by establishing a resonance pattern before these external stimuli have 'awakened' the brain and allowed it to begin to develop a distinct personality of its own, the senior may exercise *complete* mental, psychological control over the junior replicates, even when separated from them by great distances."

"An army of flesh-and-blood robots controlled by telepathy," the lord DessaTyso said. "Something the fools in power today have feared to create. Fear of the anger of the gods. Ha! More likely fear of creating a power greater than themselves."

Ignoring his lordship, AkweNema said, "Such an army we propose to give to you, Master HarkosNor."

I remembered a dream I'd once had—it now seemed like a long, long time ago—a nightmare in which I was an army of duplicate people going up against a similar army that was even greater than mine. I shuddered in remembrance of that dream, tried to push it from my mind.

"And in return for your services, HarkosNor," AkweNema was saying, "we offer you a 'time machine,' if you still want it when the victory is ours. We offer you a place in the ruling cabinet of the new NakrehVatee. We offer you wealth and power such as you might never have dreamed of before."

"You have my word on this, Master HarkosNor," the lord DessaTyso said, beaming in his magnanimity.

"And ours as well," AkweNema said.

In the pause that followed, I refilled my wineglass and drank it empty again.

"We shall not demand that you answer at once," AkweNema said. "We will give you time to think, to decide. We will not rush you, but we hope that you can see fit to join us—and soon."

"We need your help, barbarian," the dark woman OrDjina said, speaking to me as an equal, despite the title she'd just given me.

"We do indeed," her lord agreed.

I nodded, grunted, and finally spoke. "It's a tall order."

"It is late now, gentlemen, my lord, my lady," AkweNema said, "and I am certain that Master Harkos-Nor is tired." Looking at me, he said, "A suite has been made ready for you."

"And to show you that we mean you well," the lord DessaTyso said, "the first of your rewards will be waiting for you there. Is that not so, OrDjina?"

"EnDera is there, my lord, awaiting the barbarian," OrDjina said, and gave me a wicked smile, the meaning of which wasn't exactly unclear to me.

AkweNema rose to his feet, offered me his hand, and said, "Come with me, then. I will show you the way."

And as I followed AkweNema out of the luxurious suite and down the brightly lighted corridor, I hoped by all the gods of all the Earths across the Lines, including the dark ones of VarKhohs, that the Shadowy Man was really on my side this time. But hadn't he always been?

6

EnDera

The suite to which AkweNema led me was not as large as his or quite as luxuriously appointed, but there had been no stinting in it either—nor was there stinting in the first of the "rewards" offered me by the Brathel-Lanza for my future services.

The girl named EnDera was in her early twenties, with a distinctly Oriental look about her, an almost yellowishness to her skin, and epicanthic folds that gave her eyes a slightly slanted appearance. My first thought was that she might have been Japanese, but I was mistaken about that.

Her almond eyes were bright and sensual; her lips were curled in a smile; her hair was as long and as black as that of OrDjina, though it fell without curls down her back; her body was as rounded and as mature as that of the older woman, and the sight of it under the sheer, light blue gown she wore, a filmy thing more transparent than opaque, created for me nothing less than seduction. Between her breasts, visible through the fabric of her gown, dangling on a golden chain, was a looped cross of beaten gold, an ankh, an ancient symbol of life.

Had I not just met the beautiful lady OrDjina, I would have said that EnDera was easily the most beautiful woman in all VarKhohs. She was the second most beautiful, then. Who was I to complain?

AkweNema quickly made the introductions and as quickly left us, saying only that come morning we would talk again about the matter of my service to the

BrathelLanza. I agreed, but I was in no hurry for morning to come—and in no hurry to feel the pangs of guilt I would feel when I thought of Sally, so far away. . . .

"So you're the barbarian?" EnDera said in a lilting voice that carried just a trace of an accent as she sat down on the floor cushions and gestured for me to do the same. Before her sat a tall bottle of wine and two glasses.

I sat down as she poured the wine, and said, "I wish people would quit calling me that."

"Barbarian?" She handed me one of the glasses. "Well, you do speak like one. Your accent is worse than mine."

"Well, I'm sorry about that, but that doesn't make me the next best thing to a trained ape. I am housebroken, you know, and I rarely chew up people's slippers."

"I'm sorry," she said. "I didn't mean to offend you."

"You didn't really," I said. "But I'd prefer you called me Harkos." I'd really have preferred that she call me Eric, but I knew that was out of the question, and before she could say what I knew was coming next, I added, "I know that's a barbaric name too, but that's the name I've got." You pays your money and you gets potluck.

She smiled again and daintily sipped her wine.

"You're a NakrehVatea?" I asked, to break the silence that followed.

She nodded. "I was born in the West, near MaKohl. But my parents were immigrants from PalaBarhah." That was the name, Here and Now, for southern China. "We moved to VarKhohs when I was very young. I consider it my home."

"And you're a member of the BrathelLanza?" I asked, hoping I was pronouncing it correctly.

"Of course," she said, seeming surprised that I

VESTIGES OF TIME 47

should even ask. "And what of you, Harkos? What have you told them?"

I shrugged. "Nothing yet. They've given me time to think it over and make up my mind."

"I hope that you will agree to join us," she said earnestly, looking at me with a frank, open expression. "Such a man as you is needed. NakrehVatee isn't famous for its soldiers."

"Yeah, so I've gathered."

"And you would be doing the people a great service," she said just as earnestly, though not so fanatically as AkweNema might have said it. "There is much that AkweNema and KaphNo and the lord DessaTyso would do to make things better for the people, but they need help."

"Is it necessarily *my* help?"

"It could be your help. And the rewards will be great, although the knowledge that one has done the right thing should be enough." There was a gentle chiding in her voice, I thought.

"But NakrehVatee isn't my country," I told her, "and its problems aren't mine."

"Are you so much of a barbarian that you owe no debt to your fellow man?"

"I have some pressing things to attend to, EnDera. I'm not sure I can spare a year or two to assist your people."

She looked doubtfully at me. "That pressing?"

I nodded, though I wondered where I'd ever have another chance to get my hands on a time—correction, on a chronal-displacement device. I just might have to give them a year or two to get it. And maybe that's what the Shadowy Man had been hinting at.

Another thought that had been nagging just below my level of awareness surfaced now, and I put the question to her as she refilled our now-empty wine-glasses.

"Look, maybe you can answer something for me."

"I'll try."

"Well, for the sake of argument, suppose I do agree to go along and give up a couple of years of my life to help the BrathelLanza. Okay, we're speaking of maybe a year to complete the training and the preparation of the revolutionaries and then some months of fighting until the BrathelLanza has crushed all government resistance, right?"

EnDera nodded. "That's about right."

"Okay, then, how can this army of clones—replicates, whatever—that they're talking about 'growing' from cells of my body possibly be ready in time to do any good? It takes almost two decades for a human being to become anything like mature. Are they planning on sending year-old babies out to fight a war?"

She laughed, but gently. "KaphNo is getting old, Harkos. He didn't mention the GATs—growth-acceleration techniques—they've been using on animal and on some human replicates?"

"GATs?—no, I don't think so."

"He will. But it's true that the BrathelLanza now has techniques that the government's scientists and medical people know nothing about which can greatly hasten the acceleration of maturation."

"Hasten it enough to 'grow' an adult army in a year?"

"In less than a year."

"Okay," I said grudgingly.

"I'm certain that KaphNo will tell you all about it. You'll see."

I shrugged. There was a hell of a lot I had yet to learn about this world—for it was a complete world with centuries of history behind it about which I knew next to nothing, with patterns of culture I'd had only glimpses of, with technology and techniques I had encountered nowhere else across the Lines of Time. It would take a very long time for me to feel at home in it, if I ever did, and I knew I couldn't wait *that long* to make up my mind. I had to come to a decision on the basis of very scanty data and to act on that decision—and I had begun to doubt very seriously that with a negative decision on my part I would ever be allowed to leave the Underground alive. But I wasn't telling anyone anything yet.

"We want your stay here to be as pleasant as it can be," EnDera said into my silent thoughts.

"And that's why you're here, isn't it?"

She nodded. "You were told to expect a reward, weren't you?"

"I was. And you're it?"

"I'm it. Or rather the first one. There will be many more rewards, of various types, to follow, if you decide to join us."

"I'm beginning to wonder if I'm really going to be allowed any choice in the matter."

EnDera refilled both our wineglasses, took them in her hands, and rose slowly, gracefully from the floor.

"Let me show you the rest of the suite," she said as she turned her back on me, and I let my eyes follow the sweep of her dark hair down the curves of her back and hips to her ankles and feet. "It was carefully prepared for you. We hope you will find it comfortable."

She led me down a short hallway that branched off to two rooms, the one on the right a dining-room-cum-kitchen with what appeared to be automated food-preparation equipment, which she offered to show me how to operate—later. The room to the left was a study complete with a small library of books, a library of disks and tapes and playing machines for them, and one wall that was some sort of holographic-projection unit that could re-create life-size three-dimensional dramas, comedies, concerts, and readings. Again she

offered to show me how to operate the equipment—
but later.

The doors at the rear of these rooms led to hallways
that joined and then in turn branched again and led
to two more rooms, one a toilet with an enormous
sunken bathtub, more nearly a pool; the other was a
recreation room, in all appearances, fully outfitted with
games, exercise equipment, and even a rifle range.

The rear doors of these rooms led to a common hallway that finally ended in a huge bedroom—literally a
*bed*room, for its entire floor was a single great mattress
that reached from wall to wall. A mahogany-paneled
console stood in the middle of the room under a circular illumination disk surrounded by mirrors that
covered the remainder of the ceiling. EnDera didn't
have to tell me what the mirrors were for, but she did
tell me that the console was a combination wet bar,
entertainment center with holotank, and clothes closet.
She opened one panel of the console to show me the
costumes it held for me, an assortment of outfits that
included, among other things, a harshly cut uniform
that had a very, very military look about it. They were
prepared, I could say that about them, these people of
the BrathelLanza.

And so was EnDera.

"Now," she said, lowering herself to the mattress-
floor, having kicked off her shoes as we entered the
room, as I had done also, "I will try to convince you
of the wisdom of joining us."

"Okay," I said, a huskiness suddenly coming to my
throat.

She handed me one of the glasses filled with wine.
Despite all I'd already drunk that evening, I felt I
needed that one too.

"Come join *me*, Master HarkosNor," EnDera said
softly, one hand holding the wineglass, the other going
to the fasteners that held her gown together in the
back. "I think I can at least persuade you to do *that*."

The gown fell away from her breasts and crumpled around her hips. She began to work herself out of it.

"Yes, you can do that," I said, and lowered myself beside her.

She did persuade me.

7

Of Replication

When I awoke the next morning, my mouth filled with the unpleasant aftertaste and thickness of too much wine consumed the night before, and an incipient headache, I found that EnDera was way ahead of me. She had already been up for a while and there was a hot breakfast awaiting me, complete with a steaming cup of coffee—the most inviting thing I saw at the breakfast table, except for EnDera herself, who now wore only a lacy apron that was hardly a covering and couldn't have been much protection against anything, and a bright flower with yellow petals in the darkness of her long hair. Her welcoming smile was as bright as the flower she wore.

"Did you sleep well, my lord Harkos?"

"The sleep of the just and guilt-free," I said with a touch of sarcasm I don't think I really meant—at least I didn't mean for the sarcasm to be aimed at EnDera.

"What?"

"Nothing, nothing," I said, and sat down at the table, now realizing how hungry I was.

"The lord DessaTyso, AkweNema, and KaphNo will be coming to see you soon," she said as we ate. "Akwe punched up before you awoke to check on you."

I nodded, with a mouthful of food, but made no effort to speak.

"Akwe was hoping that you'd come to a decision and would speak with them of it this morning."

I nodded again, and sipped the hot coffee.

"Well, have you?"

After swallowing the coffee and gesturing for En-

Dera to refill the cup, I said: "Last night I said I didn't think I was really being given much choice in the matter."

"That's what you said."

"Well, I'm not. Am I?"

"Certainly you are. Nobody's forcing you to do anything." Was there a mocking smile barely hidden by her composed features?

"Tell me, frankly, what would happen to me if I refused."

She looked at me with a blank expression for long seconds.

I sipped hot coffee again. "Come on, tell me."

"Honestly, Harkos, I don't know, but . . ."

"Ah!" I wagged a finger at her. "If the BrathelLanza is a secret revolutionary organization, as it obviously is, and if the existing government is out to crush all such revolutionary movements, as it obviously must if it is to remain in power, then is AkweNema—the brains behind this revolution, as he seems to be—is he going to turn me, a potential government informer, loose to tell all I know to the government in possible exchange for 'rewards' from *them?*" That was some mouthful to speak that early in the morning, especially since I'd just scalded my tongue with coffee.

EnDera shook her head. "I don't know exactly what they would do in that case." Her eyes seemed to say otherwise.

"I don't know *exactly,* either, but if I were in Akwe-Nema's shoes, I could think of several things—but none of them would be very pleasant for Master HarkosNor, soldier at arms and intrepid hero."

"I see what you're saying."

"It's got to be the old carrot-and-stick game, En-Dera." I paused, gave her a long, hard, questioning look that somehow evolved into a leer. "And to tell you the truth, my dear, I much prefer the carrot to the stick, one particular carrot indeed."

At this she broke into a reluctant smile. "Then you're going to accept?"

"Like I said, do I have any choice?"

When AkweNema and KaphNo led me deeper into the underground complex of the BrathelLanza and began showing me the various parts of it, I was reminded of another underground complex on another Earth, distant across the Lines from this one, and of the people there who had also been plotting a revolution, colonial North America scheming to rise against Mother England. But that place no longer existed; destroyed by its builders to prevent its capture by the people who came to rescue me from them. And now Sally was waiting for me Somewhere Else. And I missed her and wondered when I would ever see her again.

Portions of the Underground here were devoted to offices and to sleeping quarters for both the permanently subterranean personnel and those who worked and partially lived in the world above and came into the Underground only on occasion, such as AkweNema and the lord DessaTyso, who still had active parts to play in the society of the surface. Farther back, the offices and quarters gave way to supply dumps, to equipment and matériel they were slowly collecting, building, enlarging, in preparation for the day when the BrathelLanza and its allies would come out of their hidden places and attack the power structure that ruled NakrehVatee.

Still farther on were large, brightly lighted exercise areas and drill fields carved out of the earth and stone, in which was completed the training of the cadres that would soon issue forth to begin the training of others around the nation. The uniforms they wore, the men and women who were presently the crack forces of the BrathelLanza, were not greatly unlike those worn by the armies of many another world: blouses and slacks of tan—khaki, the word was in some places—metal helmets, heavy boots; and the weapons with which they exercised were bright and sparkling, highly sophisticated automatic rifles and pistols capable of throwing leaden slugs or explosive shells great distances with a high degree of accuracy, compact particle-beam weapons and hand-held lasers capable of projecting fragments of shattered atoms, electrons, protons, beams of coherent light and heat. Unfortunately, however, the soldiers were not as sophisticated as their weapons. But then, I suppose, that's why they wanted someone like me.

And beyond the training areas lay the biological laboratories. This was where I would be occupied initially. Only later would I be spending the bulk of my time in the training areas, drilling *my* troops and advising the training of others.

We entered the bright, antiseptic labs, smelled the clean, almost sterile air, watched the efficient movements of the physicians and scientists and technicians as they went about their esoteric business—esoteric to me; but now I could see that old KaphNo was finally in his element. He seemed a different man, alive, excited, animated by his love for the laboratories and what was taking place in them.

"Everything is ready for you, Master HarkosNor— or should I say 'General' HarkosNor?" KaphNo said, beaming at me. "We could even begin today if you wish." He paused for a moment, ruminated. "We have several human replicates, which you will see later, in various stages of maturation, developing with no indication of trouble.

"In fact," he said, speaking more slowly, more emphatically, "we even have several fully matured replicates living in the Underground now. You would not be able to distinguish them from other people—in fact, I'll see that you meet one of them soon, and you can see for yourself what I mean.

"Yes, all in all, everything is proceeding even better than we had expected. We anticipate no problems in cloning several hundred replicates from the cells of your tissues."

"That's very good," AkweNema said, a strange, uneasy expression passing across his face. "Perhaps ThefeRa could give the general a tour of the replication facilities."

"Of course," KaphNo said, and gestured toward two white-clad men who stood discussing something at a table not far away.

The two men joined us and were introduced. The elder, a tall, thin, almost cadaverous man with a great shock of white hair, was named ThefeRa and was both a physician and a microbiologist specializing in replication processes: in short, a "genetic engineer." He was, under KaphNo, the project's head.

The other, a shorter, heavier, young man, with unusually handsome features, was named SkorTho. He also was a microbiologist and served as ThefeRa's second in command.

When the introductions were completed, ThefeRa led us into the section of the laboratories that was to be of particular interest to me.

"This is our operating room," the white-haired physician said, gesturing with his left hand toward a large set of white doors. He glanced at AkweNema and KaphNo, then back at me, and said: "When you are ready, General, it is here that we will take the sample tissues from which your replicates will be grown."

"A painless operation, I assure you," AkweNema put in, sounding like the physician he was. "A simple biopsy, a few thousand cells you'll never miss. That's all."

I shrugged.

Farther on: ThefeRa gesturing, speaking. "In these rooms the cells we will have taken from your body will be placed in special media which will provide them with ample nutrition and in which they will be encouraged to grow, to reproduce. At this stage, all we want is to establish that the cells will breed true—that is, skin cells produce more skin cells, muscle cells more muscle cells, whatever."

"In essence," KaphNo interjected, "the sample cells from your body will be encouraged to reproduce themselves a number of times over, so that when we are finished here we will have a much larger amount of tissue with which to work."

It all sounded rather grotesque to me, and I wasn't certain that I wanted to see that actual process. I mean, that would be *my* tissue, all raw and naked, growing like the still-beating heart of some long-dead chicken. Ugh!

"Not so long ago," KaphNo was saying into my gruesome thoughts, "the process of developing a viable replicate was a much more complex and less trustworthy operation. We have refined and simplified the process greatly here in recent years, thanks largely to the efforts of ThefeRa and SkorTho."

The two genetic engineers somehow managed to look both humble and proud at the same time.

"Not so long ago," KaphNo continued, "we could reproduce only viable female replicates by a rather messy and involved process which involved the transplantation of a cell nucleus from the body of a donor into a fertilized egg cell from which the nucleus had been removed, and then this egg had to be implanted into the womb of a surrogate mother."

Looking proud of himself and his co-workers, the old scientist said, "Well, now we have been able to bypass the egg-cell implant stage and the surrogate mother altogether. We can persuade an even rather specialized cell to develop embryonically. The womb of the surrogate mother has been replaced by something that I can only call a marvel of engineering. You will see what I'm referring to shortly."

"The next step," ThefeRa said into the silence following the end of KaphNo's speech, gesturing toward another pair of white doors, "once we have what we feel to be a sufficient culture to work with, will be the separation of individual cells from the clone mass. That's where the word 'clone' comes from, you know, a Greek word meaning 'throng.' We apply it to a heterogeneous mass of genetically identical cells."

"I know," I said, not mentioning that a version of the Greek language had been my native tongue. They didn't need to know *that*.

"And that is why," KaphNo said, "we prefer the word 'replicate' to 'clone' when speaking of the *individual* produced by this process."

I nodded, understanding.

"Once replication has sucessfully begun," the physician ThefeRa continued, "the embryos—for at this stage they can be considered embryos, having no zygotic stage in the true sense of the term—are transferred to another room. For the first few days the embryonic replicates are kept under constant surveillance. At this stage we lose about one out of every three embryos."

"Lose?" I asked, unable to constrain myself. I was getting curious about this whole thing; after all, weren't they going to grow some new *me*s here?

KaphNo answered: "This science is still in its infancy, General. And it is here in this room that we must catch the bulk of our mistakes. Faulty stimulation of genetic patterns. Failure of replication processes. Mutations—even underground here there's more radiation than we would like. Other genetic defects caused by the very methods we are using. One third of the embryos we bring into this room are not suitable for further cultivation. By the time the embryos leave this room, we will have lost seven out of every

eight of the cells we started with. That is why we need
a relatively large number of cells initially."

Again I felt that tug of revulsion. Maybe I didn't
have as strong a stomach as I'd thought.

"At the end of this stage, however," ThefeRa picked
up the narrative, "we can be certain of the survival of
a large percentage of the embryos. From here they will
be transferred to the room ahead and on our right,
where we can begin to apply certain growth-acceleration techniques we have developed that will . . ."

On and on we went, from room to room, lab to lab,
ThefeRa and KaphNo leading, AkweNema and I behind, the microbiologist SkorTho silently bringing up
the rear. And as we went I was shown the various
stages of growth through which the replicates would
pass, was shown various human replicates in the actual
process of growth and development, spanning years of
maturation in days.

"We have three types of vessels for the postnatal replicates," said ThefeRa at one point. "We have coined
the word 'encanter' for the replication vessels, which you
are about to see. The smallest of these are for replicates with a chronological maturity from 'birth' up to
six years."

An encanter, it turned out, was something like a
cross between a Skinner box and an overgrown test tube
and looked something like a deranged chemist's idea
of a tropical-fish aquarium.

ThefeRa led us into a long, low room, the walls of
which were lined with glass cylinders each about four
feet tall and two feet in diameter. Beside each cylinder
was a large electronic console more complex than the
controls of a good-size cargo skudder, with banks of
dials, gauges, meters, buttons, switches, and CRTs. The
cylinders themselves were topped by large metal rings
from which tubes or pipes ran back into boxes and
junctions in the wall. From the bases of the cylinders
similar tubes ran into similar boxes and junctions at

the bases of the consoles. In all there appeared to be several hundred of these cylinder-console combinations. The cost must have been enormous.

Then ThefeRa led us down the row of cylinders until he reached one that stood a hundred feet or so from the door through which we'd entered.

"This should prove interesting to you," he said, gesturing for me to come nearer.

Before I even reached ThefeRa, several things about this particular setup became obvious to me. Initially: the console that stood beside and was connected to the cylinder was not dark and quiet as had been the others —its panels were lighted, tiny indicator lights flickered on and off, meters showed various readings, and the console itself hummed with electrical life. Next: the cylinder beside the console was less transparent than the others, filled with a thick, murky fluid that seemed to be in constant motion.

"See him?" ThefeRa asked.

I bent slightly, peered into the cylinder. I saw him.

The form of a naked boy of about five years old hung/swam suspended in the liquid, long, dark hair swaying in the gentle motion of the cylinder's fluid contents. His eyes were closed, and my first impression was that he was dead—a grotesque display of child murder committed by some maddened scientist of the underground laboratories. Then I saw that his chest rose and fell with a slow but unmistakable rhythm.

"The liquid in which he floats contains oxygen which the lungs are capable of extracting," ThefeRa said, seeing the look in my eyes. "He is alive and well, developing physiologically normally in almost every way."

"Except for the rate of growth," KaphNo said, coming up behind me. "We began the replication process eight weeks ago, and now he shows a maturation of about five and a third years."

"How—how long," I stammered, "how long until he's, ah, mature?"

"We will able to carry him to a maturation level of eighteen years over a period of just less than ten months. But don't try to work out the direct chronological equivalents in normal maturity. There is not a one-to-one congruity. Some stages we can accelerate more, some less."

I nodded, too flooded with information to speak at that moment, and in my silence the scientists led me on down the row of encanters and showed me the two "brothers" of the boy—two more replicates genetically identical with the first, triplets growing in the laboratories of the BrathelLanza deep beneath the surface of the Earth.

I was not told their names—if they yet had names —or who had donated the cells from which they were growing. Perhaps it wasn't important.

Then we went on to the next set of encanters, larger than the first, designed to hold replicates from maturation levels of about six years to about twelve years. In one of these I was shown what ThefeRa called "one of our happier replications"—a naked, black-haired girl who somehow looked astonishingly familiar, floating, sleeping in the murky liquid.

"Don't you recognize her?" ThefeRa asked.

"Yes . . . yes, I think so."

"Little OrDjina," KaphNo said with a laugh, "that's what we call her. And as you can easily see, she is a replication of our lord DessaTyso's mistress. A beautiful child, isn't she?"

I nodded but couldn't find words to speak.

"On the day of her final decantation, a little over four months from now," ThefeRa was saying, "a celebration is planned. That should be interesting— two Ladies OrDjina in our Underground."

I wondered exactly what he meant by that, but I didn't ask.

Finally we followed ThefeRa to the last of the encanter chambers, a room which held the largest cylinders of all, those built to hold replicates at maturation levels from twelve years to maturity. Only one of these encanters was occupied; it held the form of a lovely young girl of about fifteen, her hair a startling shade of red.

AkweNema, without speaking, brushed around the rest of us and took a place directly in front of the large glass cylinder. For a long while he gazed silently into the murky fluid. There appeared to be moisture in the corners of his eyes. No one spoke.

Finally he turned awkwardly from the encanter, and faced us, his eyes seeking mine. He spoke: "My daughter." Then he left the encanter room alone and went back toward the other sections of the Underground, muttering something to himself that may have been "May the Dark Lords have mercy on us all."

ThefeRa was the first to speak. "His true daughter is dead. A tragic skimmer accident a few months ago. She was almost sixteen years old, just a bit more mature than her replicate here. We were able to retrieve some still-living cells and are growing this replicate for Akwe. She will reach maturation in about two months if we continue the process."

"But that's not enough," KaphNo said, an unexpected softness in his voice, an affection for the red-haired man and his dead daughter. "If only we had complete cerebral recordings of her! With those we could give him back his daughter just as she was."

Huh? I asked, but silently, to myself.

Old KaphNo turned, wiped incipient tears from his eyes, grasped my upper arm with a surprisingly strong hand, and led me out of the encanter chamber.

"Cerebral recordings, General. I haven't spoken of them, have I?" he asked when we were again in the corridor.

"No, you haven't."

"Well then, it's time I told you about them. They

play a very important part in our plan. Now, I am certain that you are familiar with the fact that the human brain constantly gives off certain forms of electromagnetic emissions, brain waves, the so-called alpha waves and so forth; that is to say . . ."

8

Of the Underground

That night I lay in the room-filling bed beside EnDera, both of us warm and satiated, drifting toward a welcome sleep—or at least EnDera seemed to be. I wanted to sleep but found it impossible. There was too much in my head. Clones and replication processes. Brain waves and cerebral-recording techniques. Replicates of the lord DessaTyso's beautiful mistress and of AkweNema's dead daughter floating in tanks of life-supporting fluids. The identical boys in similar encanters. Wars and rumors of wars in a world the complexities of which I could not yet begin to understand. The vast underground city of the BrathelLanza—for it was almost a city in size and complexity, similar in some respects to the underground city-fortress of the Paratimers and the American Republican Army on another Earth.

And that similarity with the place called Staunton disturbed me. Not similarity in detail, for there was little or none of that. But in scope and concept, in size and complexity, and especially in purpose. Staunton and *this* Underground, so similar in many general ways, had both been built for the purpose of overthrowing the existing power structure and replacing it with another.

The Paratimers—whatever the hell they *were,* and I didn't know—had financed and helped build the underground city of Staunton.

What of the underground city of the BrathelLanza? . . .

I supposed that EnDera needed the sleep—she had

earned it well during our romp on the great mattress, earned it every bit as well as the EstarSimirian prostitutes earned theirs in the pleasure-house in VarKhohs —but I had to talk with someone, and she was the most available. I rolled over, touched her cheek with my fingertips, and whispered into her ear, "EnDera, EnDera."

"What is it?" she asked sleepily.

"Would you mind staying awake just a little while longer? I'd like to talk."

A frown crossed her lovely face in the room's dim light. "Is something bothering you?"

"This place, this Underground, I can't figure it out."

"What do you mean?"

"Well, I mean I'm impressed and all. I've never seen anything like it." Which wasn't exactly the truth, but close enough to it. "It's hard to imagine how something like this could have been built, and all this equipment and all these people brought in, without anyone knowing about it."

"Oh, lots of people know about it."

"That's not what I mean. The government. How is it that they didn't learn about it long ago?"

"Oh, I'm sure a number of people in the government have known about it. Never the top people, of course, but a lot of people lower down the line. It's been seen to that they never pass their information on to the top."

"What do you mean 'seen to'?"

"Oh, a few bribes strategically placed, maybe a little extortion, maybe a little blackmail, maybe an 'unfortunate accident' here and there."

"I see." Maybe the BrathelLanza wasn't just *playing* at revolution after all. Maybe they were deadly serious. Assassination. That's deadly serious.

"I can't say that we're entirely safe here," EnDera went on. "Sooner or later some overly zealous agent is going to put two and two together and come up with the right answer and we won't be able to stop him from alerting the ones on the top, but we hope that day can be put off long enough for us to finish our work here."

I nodded, understanding.

"Really, Harkos, we don't have too many illusions down here. We know we're under sentences of immediate execution on the spot, or prolonged torture in some of the lords' dungeons, if we're ever caught. We just hope we can put off being caught for a few more months."

There was a coldness in her eyes and in her words that showed me a new side of EnDera and maybe a new side of this whole underground setup.

"That's one of the reasons we were in such a rush to get your cooperation," she went on, her fingers unconsciously touching the looped cross of life she wore. "Don't flatter yourself by thinking you're the only man in the world we could use. There are lots of others. We even have some people in our organization now who could serve in your place in a pinch. But you're the most available of the best suited, if you follow me."

"And this business this morning when I asked you what they would do if I refused?"

"I know. I guess I was playing with you. But I didn't want you to agree unless you wanted to cooperate. I didn't want to scare you into it. But . . . but you're right. If you hadn't agreed this morning, you would probably be dead by now. I'm glad you agreed."

"I am too."

A long, quiet pause followed while I framed questions in my mind, working out a means of getting from her the kinds of answers I wanted.

"This place must have cost a fortune to build, several fortunes. Who's paying for it?"

"A lot of people, an awful lot of people, Harkos. The lord DessaTyso and his family, for example. They've come close to destituting themselves to aid us. He's the most wealthy of us, of course, but a lot of other people in the higher castes—people as fed up with things as we are—have helped us, have given us every bit of aid they could.

"And it's not just rich people, either. Poor- and middle-caste people all over the nation have chipped in what they could to help us—and in a lot of cases, maybe in most of them, they didn't even know what they were giving their money to, but they were told that they were working for the good of all the people. And that was the truth."

She wasn't as fanatic as AkweNema, maybe, but there was a dedication in her that burned like a bright fire.

"We have other friends too."

My heart skipped a beat. *Other friends?*

"People and organizations outside NakrehVatee," she said, answering my unvoiced question. "Other governments. Private organizations. Wealthy individuals. A lot of people think the world would be better off if there were a different kind of government here in Var-Khohs.

"And maybe some of them aren't so friendly. Maybe they'd like nothing better than to see internal turmoil paralyze NakrehVatee so they could go about their business without the interference of our government. Okay, we'll take their money and their aid. But we're not committing ourselves to anything or anyone outside the BrathelLanza." Where had I heard similar sentiments expressed before? "We're not going to stage our revolution so that some other nation can jump into an international power vacuum and start dominating the small nations in our sphere of influence. That's one thing we're not going to do. We'll keep up our nation's strength against foreign powers."

I wasn't certain that I followed her line of reasoning, but that's not what was coming to concern me right at that moment. "Other friends," she had said, and those two words led me to think about the world in which I had found myself, how I had come there, why I had come there; to think of the Kriths and the Tromas who directed them and what they had said that had led me to the world of the BrathelLanza and NakrehVatee. "Other friends" seemed to abound.

And I was remembering some words spoken to me some months before by a gross and alien female Krith. The words came clearly into my mind as if I were listening to a recording of that conversation:

"There is another falsehood," the speaker for the Tromas had said to me, "that you and countless others have come to accept, a falsehood which has been 'proved' mathematically to a vast number of scientists."

"And what's that?" I'd asked.

"That travel through time is impossible, travel from one point in time to an earlier point in time."

I had just looked at the female Krith.

"Time travel *is* possible, Eric, travel from one location in *linear* time to another location, future and/or past. It is something we do not wish to become common knowledge. It is a secret *we* must keep, at the peril of our racial lives."

And later on in that same, long conversation:

"How it was we discovered the one Timeline that had achieved true time travel," she had said, "I will not go into, nor how it was that we, our entire race, migrated back in time hundreds of years in order to begin our 'remodeling' as early as possible. You must merely accept these things as so, as you have seen for yourself."

All this was clear in my mind, and the realization that the operative sentence was: *It is a secret we must keep, at the peril of our racial lives.*

This was that world, the one with true time travel, I was almost certain, and if that were so, then there could be no chance of the Kriths having allowed Paratimers *or anyone else* to have infiltrated this world, to have financed and assisted with the planning of a revolution that would probably drastically alter the government of this Earth's most powerful nation. Nor would the Kriths or the Timeliners meddle with this world, but merely stand outside it and make certain no one else did.

(How, then, did you get into this world so easily? a portion of my mind asked. They should have been watching for exactly the thing you did—a stranger coming skudding in to make use of this Line's "time machines." They should have caught you. If this *is* the right world . . .)

And again: If this is the right world, if I haven't made a terrible blunder, then would the Kriths allow even the natives of this world, the BrathelLanza and people like them, to make drastic alterations in its historical processes?

(And another part of my mind: But the Shadowy Man wouldn't have advised you to cooperate with the BrathelLanza, to allow them to clone your cells and to have you lead an army of replicates so that when the revolution is all over you can get your hands on a chronal-displacement device, if this is the wrong world. The Shadowy Man is on your side. Isn't he?)

And again: But if the revolution is staged and executed solely by natives without any Outtime activities involved at all, would not that revolution be a part of that world's natural historical process, something that must have happened here if the future is to turn out as the Kriths see it?

(But there is an Outtime influence! You!)

But the Kriths don't know it, do they?

(They should.

(If you're on the right world.

(If you haven't made the worst blunder of your life.

(If the Shadowy Man isn't playing you for a fool.

(If . . .)

EnDera was looking at me strangely but didn't speak. She had had her say.

So I just kissed her, and she returned the kiss, and I pulled her naked body closer to mine and kissed her again and for a while I forgot about all those things running through my head. For a while . . .

9

A Conversation with KaphNo

Although AkweNema, KaphNo, ThefeRa, and a score
of others had insisted that the taking of the tissue
sample from my body would be absolutely painless,
I discovered that they had stretched the point just a
bit. Oh, the taking of the sample itself was painless
enough, I admit. I was given a local anesthetic in my
left hip, placed on something that looked like a hybrid
of a conventional operating table and a dentist's chair,
had a strap placed across my chest, and ThefeRa himself—I should consider this an honor, I was told—
placed a device against the outside of my left thigh,
which sent a small, circular blade about an inch into
my flesh, taking out a core a few millimeters in diameter of skin and flesh and muscle tissue. During the
taking of the biopsy, KaphNo, who stood at my left
hand, told me the approximate number of cells that
would be removed, but I've forgotten how many he
said. Sufficiently large for their purposes, with a good
loss factor figured in.

The biopsy was over in a matter of minutes and the
small wound in my thigh was closed and sealed with
something I would have called "plastiskin." They
wouldn't let me try to walk until the anesthetic had
worn off, but when it had I didn't much want to walk
anyway. That's what they hadn't told me about: once
the anesthetic wore off, it did hurt terribly for a while.
You know how puncture wounds are. But I didn't complain to anyone. Generals don't cry, do they?

I spent the rest of that day, my second full day in
the Underground of the BrathelLanza, resting in the

"study" of my suite, using the equipment that EnDera had finally shown me how to work, sipping cold beer —they brewed some fine beer Here and Now—smoking cigarettes, which I'd finally been able to obtain— the use of tobacco being almost unknown in NakrehVatee—and skimming through the spools of an encyclopedia, familiarizing myself with the more salient facts about the city of VarKhohs, the nation of NakrehVatee, and the world of which they were a part.

This world, I determined, was one of a series of related Timelines that the Kriths collectively called Neo-Carthaginian. Carthage. In the Phoenician, *Kart Hadasht*. In the Greek of my ancestors, *Karchedon*. The Jewel of North Africa. The Mother of Kings—in this world at least.

In the history of these so-called Neo-Carthaginian worlds, the tactics of the great general Hannibal had been more successful than on many another Line. Iberia had remained in the hands of Carthage during the Second Punic War. Hannibal crossed the Alps and fell on Rome with all his fury. And it had been the Romans, in the year B.C. 200, who had gone down in flames, not the descendants of the Phoenicians.

Rome was leveled and her colonies taken over by the Carthaginians. Though later rebuilt as a satellite of Carthage and renamed, the city of Rome never gained great importance outside the Italian peninsula. The centers of power remained in the Near East and the Far East, moving to Europe only centuries later when it too was colonized and dominated by Asiatic and African peoples who had risen to power following the fall of the Cartho-Byzantine Empire.

All this, in much more detail, I learned as I read books and scanned tapes that day, relaxing and attempting to enjoy myself.

Late that evening, after sharing a large meal with EnDera, which she'd prepared with aid from the auto-kitchen, I was paid a visit by Professor KaphNo, who now seemed to be a rather happy, animated old man.

"Well, Master Harkos, we have begun," he said, sitting on a cushion across from me, gazing into the foam in his mug of beer, which EnDera had also provided.

"The replication?" I asked.

"Not the replication exactly, but the first stages of cloning that will lead to replication. Your cells have been placed in the growth media and are already beginning to respond. We should have an ample quantity of cells to begin the actual replication processes by the end of the week, I would say."

"And then?"

The bright eyes in the deep sockets sparkled. "Then . . . well, in about ten months, General, you should have your army."

"The replicates will be mature then?"

He nodded. "There are some other things you should keep in mind, however."

"Okay."

"When the replicates reach a maturation level equivalent to eighteen years of age—ML-18Y, that's the way we say it in the labs—they will be ready to be decanted. However, you cannot expect them to be able to immediately function as would a normal human being. Their muscles will have a lot of developing yet to do. Although they will have been fed certain data during the last weeks of their development—data concerning the use of their muscles—much of this data cannot be fully integrated by them until after decanting. What I am saying, Harkos, is that it will take the replicates several weeks to *learn to use* their bodies, to be anything more than helpless babies."

I nodded over the top of my own beer mug.

"Also, during the last few weeks of their development prior to decanting, they will have been carefully fed certain portions of your cerebral recordings. That is, with your assistance, during the recording, the edit-

ing, and the playback, we will want to feed your replicates that data from your memories which is felt to be
of value to them."

"I think I follow you," I said, "but I'm not altogether certain. Now I'm supposed to have this, well,
telepathic control over—"

KaphNo raised a hand to interrupt. "We prefer the
term 'resonance.' In your case, resonance control.
'Telepathy' is such a sloppy term."

I recalled another being in another place who had
said how sloppy were human terms for psionic effects.
I guess she was right.

"You will be expected to exercise resonance control
over the replicates. They, in turn, will follow your
commands in terms of resonance *response.*"

"Okay," I agreed. "This resonance control I'll have
over them—won't that make it possible for them to do
anything I tell them without their having, well, personalities of their own?"

"That would hardly be practical, Harkos," KaphNo
said flatly, perhaps doubting my understanding of any
of it. "We are talking about *several hundred* replicates.
Of course, you could personally direct one or even two
to a very large degree, but to control even two well,
or three or four in any fashion at all, would be a full-
time job. You would have to be placed in a sensory-
deprived situation and then spend all your waking
hours flitting from one subject to another, directing its
every task.

"No, Harkos," he said loudly, "you are to be the
general of hundreds, not the *puppet master* of a handful. Your replicates will have, to a limited degree, of
course, distinct memory patterns, distinct experience
programs, distinct behavior patterns—in short, for
want of a better term, personalities. Your control over
them will be of a more general, over-all fashion.

"Here's the way you'll do it: 'Harkos R52, take six
men and try to knock out that guard post on the next

street. Harkos R87's platoon will converge with your detail and together you will go to the assistance of Harkos R210 two blocks to the north.' That, Harkos, is the way you will direct your troops."

I leaned back, smiled, sipped my beer to the bottom of the mug, then called EnDera and asked her to please get us both a refill.

"Do you understand the distinctions now?" KaphNo asked, sitting down.

"I think I'm beginning to, but tell me, just how does this resonance business work—no, how will it *seem to me?* I guess is what I'm asking."

"I don't think I can give you a definitive answer to that as yet. Oh, thank you." EnDera had brought us the beer. "Never before has anyone attempted resonance control with so many replicates. Experience in the past has dealt with no more than two or three replicates and their senior. But we know there are three levels of integration with your replicates.

"RCL One—RCL stands for resonance-control level —RCL One would probably very closely coincide with your normal, waking, conscious operation. You will be very much 'in your own head,' as it were, and your directing of the replicates would be very analogous with the way a conventional commander in the field directs his troops: he uses radio and/or video; whereas you will be, well, directing by means of your thoughts, so to speak, your 'sympathetic awareness.' We doubt that this will be greatly taxing, and you should be able to master it quite easily, almost instinctively, one might say.

"RCL Two we consider an intermediate stage. In it, which would require slightly greater mental concentration, you would be directing your attention to one or a few replicates, more fully aware of their thoughts and activities, of their sensory input, but hardly fully integrated with them.

"RCL Three will probably be the most difficult to

adjust to, for in it you would be allowing your response patterns—your *self,* your *soul,* if you feel poetically inclined—to fully mesh with that of a single replicate." He spread the fingers of his thin hands and then brought them together so that the fingers of one hand entwined with those of the other, mating with one another like the teeth of cog wheels. "At RCL Three you would be able to see through the replicate's eyes, hear with his ears, taste with his tongue, even speak with his vocal cords—and, of course, experience his pain. In essence, you and he would be a single person inhabiting two bodies.

"We do not believe that it will be necessary for you to use RCL Three to any great extent. In fact, we advise against it."

"I see."

"The training, as you can see," he went on after a moment, "will not be all on the part of the replicates. You yourself will have a great deal to learn in the process."

I nodded dismally. Maybe it wasn't going to be the sinecure I had thought it would be.

"But I am certain you will find it interesting and rewarding," KaphNo said, as if to cheer me up.

"Tell me about this cerebral-recording business," I said, my mouth damp with beer and foam. "You explained to me about the so-called brain waves and all that, and I think I've got some idea of what you're doing when you're making these recordings—"

"Essentially similar to the recording of any electromagnetic phenomenon," KaphNo interjected, "but the modulation end of it is a lot more sophisticated."

"So you told me. But what am I going to be doing while all this is going on?"

KaphNo smiled one of those rare smiles of his, stretched, drank beer, relaxed, and said, "We are getting a little out of my field. This is more in psychologist GrelLo's domain, but I'll tell you what I can.

"The recordings will be accomplished through several phases, as I think I mentioned to you earlier. First of all, before any actual recordings are made, you will make up what we call a 'mnemonic autobiograph,' with GrelLo's help, of course. Your life experiences will then be broken down into a number of clearly defined categories—any of which you consider of a highly personal or private nature and/or nonrelevant to our training purposes will be struck from the initial records. Prying into your personal life will be avoided as far as possible. She and her technicians will go after the specific memory types desired."

After calling to EnDera for still another refill of our beer mugs, I asked, "How is this done?"

"During the recording sessions, which GrelLo will supervise, you will be given drugs to help you relax and to facilitate memory retrieval. Half a dozen or so electrodes will be placed at various spots on your scalp and the back of your neck. That's all. Very much like an EEG, if you've ever had one. The machines and the computers do the rest."

"And after the memories are recorded?"

"They will be played back to you in a shorthand fashion and you will be given the opportunity to edit them before GrelLo and her staff further edit them. After that, the tapes will be ready to be played to your replicates."

"Well, it doesn't sound like there's anything to be afraid of there," I said, wondering if that was true. How great a chance was there that I might give myself away as not being what I claimed to be? I'd have to play that carefully indeed.

KaphNo was giving me another of his smiles. "As if there were much you have ever feared, my general."

"Don't overrate me, KaphNo. I'm no superhuman warrior out of some Norse saga. Just a simple soldier."

"No longer that. Not when you have an army that will literally obey your slightest whim."

"That does scare me a little."

"It shouldn't. You have the capacity to handle it."

"I hope you're right."

"This isn't something we've undertaken lightly. We know what kind of man you are, HarkosNor, otherwise we wouldn't have chosen you."

Do you really? I asked myself. And was hit by a sudden feeling of chill: What if they *did know?* What if they knew who and what I really was?

(Maybe they do know, said that cantankerous part of my mind. Maybe they've known all along.)

And thoughts like that could have led me down the dark paths I'd followed the night before, down into plots within plots within plots, and I wasn't ready for all that again.

"Are you feeling well?" KaphNo asked.

"I'm okay. I think I ate too much for supper. A touch of indigestion."

"Should I call EnDera? She could get you something."

"No, I'm fine now. Would you like another beer?"

We each had another, and then another, and before the evening was over KaphNo was weeping like a baby, telling me about a sweetheart he'd once had, long ago, the most beautiful girl he'd ever seen, and how he'd lost her to another.

EnDera was already asleep when I groggily crawled into the room that was a bed. I didn't bother to wake her. We both needed the sleep.

10
Of EnDera and KaphNo

Within the crystalline vessels called encanters, the manipulated and irradiated cells whose DNA carried data identical to that within my body began to grow and divide, and grow and divide again, in a fashion very similar to that which takes place within a mother's womb. Cells that had originally been unspecialized began to differentiate and develop particular characteristics the parent cells had not had. Still hardly more than microscopic, within the embryos, the rudiments of organs—heart, liver, brain, lungs, digestive tract—began to take shape. In the murky fluid of the encanters the masses of cells curved, fattened, backbones began to grow, and the buds that would later be arms and legs began to sprout. Not yet did they look even vaguely human, but the indications were there if you knew how to look for them. With the passage of days, of weeks, the cells continued to grow, to change, to become. . . .

As the embryos within the replication encanters in the laboratories of the Underground evolved through recapitulation toward "birth," which for them would consist of no more than being placed in larger encanters where most of the organs and much of the tissue of their bodies would begin to function in more nearly normal fashion, I was going through some processes myself.

With a voice recorder, a note pad, and a pencil, with the help of psychologist GrelLo—a rather mature woman, attractive, and not unpleasant to work with— I was putting together what they called a mnemonic autobiograph, but which was more nearly a quickly sketched outline of the principal memories of my life and the structure of my life as I saw it in retrospect— which was one hell of a thing to do, since I had to make up a lot of it as I went along.

As far as possible I used real events from my past, modifying the suitable ones to fit into the patterns of this world as I knew them. Claiming to be a foreigner, born and raised in the Central European country of SteeMehseeh, helped in covering some of my fabrications—but not much.

However, GrelLo didn't seem to be as much interested in my life itself as she was interested in categories of memories, my "epistemological mnemology," she called it: the taxonomy of my mind. She wanted to know how I classified my thoughts and memories, to determine what categories were relevant to the clones —excuse me, the replicates—and to determine how best to call up those specific memories for recording.

For example, she didn't much care when or where or how I'd learned to operate and maintain an automatic slug-throwing rifle, but she did want to know and to record everything I had ever known about the subject itself. My personal feelings about slug throwers and the experiences I'd had with them were irrelevant, or at best secondary, unless they told how to use and maintain a slug thrower in the field, how to load and fire with accuracy under real combat conditions. This saved me a lot of embarrassment, and from their discovery of my falsified past. Or so it seemed at the time . . .

By the time the replicates could justifiably be called "babies" and had been placed in the "newborn" encanters, GrelLo and her assistants and technicians had already begun to record my memories.

When I wasn't in session with GrelLo and her people, or in conference with TheFeRa and his people—

for I had a lot to learn before I could ever hope to begin training the replicates—or in conference with AkweNema and the lord DessaTyso—learning the ins and outs of the BrathelLanza, the breadth and depth of the organization, their plans, their goals, the structure of their organization and the structure of the organiza- tion to which they were opposed, and, of course, the tactical and strategic goals of the revolution in military terms—when I wasn't involved in these things, all of which consumed large chunks of time, I furthered my own education with the tapes and disks and books in the suite they'd given me, and called upon the Under- ground's central library computer, and, on occasion, I spent a little time with EnDera, for she would live in my suite for as long as I wished, and with KaphNo, who was becoming almost a friend.

Of the two, I'm not certain which was the less com- plex person. Perhaps it was EnDera. A beautiful, in- telligent girl she certainly was, and one whose parents, foreigners themselves, had tried to raise as a normal citizen of NakrehVatee. They had come from southern China, immigrants to North America who, because of their background in their native land, were allowed to enter one of the higher middle castes devoted to artistic endeavors. EnDera had done much the same things as other girls of her caste and social status, gone through the same sort of training and education, the same in- troductions to their segment of society, to their pre- scribed version of life and love and sexual experience, for within certain caste-limited bounds, the society of NakrehVatee was rather permissive sexually. But there had always been a difference for EnDera: she wasn't quite like her peers, her skin wasn't the same darkish color, nor her hair the same texture, nor were her eyelids shaped the same. And for those reasons, and for some others, neither did she think in the same ways.

After completing her education in the arts, hoping

that her parentage and her Oriental ancestry would give her the mastery of brush and pen for which "China" had long been famous in this world, she found that this did not satisfy her, and ultimately, after some initial successes, she largely gave up her painting and began to devote herself to revolutionary activities— for which she was eventually jailed and given psychiatric treatment. The treatment failed to change her views, although she simulated recantation sufficiently to be released. Upon her release she immediately sought out the strongest revolutionary movement of them all, the almost legendary BrathelLanza. In the Brotherhood she found the acceptance that had so long been denied her. Now she lived full time in the Underground, going to the surface only on occasion, working again as an artist and designer—not such a strange occupation for a revolutionary, if you think about it. Part of her artistic efforts were devoted to the design and execution of posters thought up by the BrathelLanza's propaganda department—the leaders of the Brotherhood knew the necessity of getting their message across to the masses. The rest of her efforts were spent on more innocuous types of art, these to be sold through the art galleries of VarKhohs and the profits channeled into the treasury of the BrathelLanza. The mysterious artist who signed her delicate, almost esoteric works merely "ED" had become something of a rage among certain castes of the city who took seriously the collecting of art. EnDera also worked in other capacities for the Brotherhood, one of which was as companion and mistress to a newly appointed general, a barbarian with the outlandish name of HarkosNor.

"And you're happy living like this?" I asked her once as she sat before her easel, a watercolor landscape ablaze with bright flowers evolving under the deft strokes of her brush.

"Happy?" she said, pausing to dip her brush in clear water. "I don't usually think of myself in those terms, but—well, I suppose I am, as happy as I can be in the world the way it is. Someday, perhaps . . ."

"Someday?" I repeated, making the word a question.

"Someday the world will be different and I will be free and happy in it. When that day comes, everyone in NakrehVatee will be happy." Her brush moved toward the ceramic palette and a pool of brilliant yellow color.

"Everyone but the ones we"—I now used the first-person plural when speaking of the BrathelLanza— "throw out of their positions of wealth and power, is that right?"

"Well, of course *they* won't be happy. But they've had their day. Like the dinosaurs. And they'll be extinct too."

A yellow flower blossomed on the rough texture of the watercolor paper.

"But everyone else will be happy?" I asked.

"I certainly hope so."

"And what about you?"

"Isn't that what I said?" She rinsed the brush in clean water. "I'll be happy then. I'll have done my job." There was an angry, disturbed look in her eyes as she dipped the brush into a green pool and then began to paint a stem and leaves for the still-wet yellow flower.

I said no more. Maybe I'd already said too much.

But I wondered.

What does a born revolutionary do when all the revolutions are over?

Well, there's always another government to overthrow somewhere else, I suppose.

As for old KaphNo, except for bits and pieces I'd gathered here and there, mostly when he was rather deep in his cups, his life was a closed book. What had changed him from a satisfied member of one of the higher and more affluent castes to an almost fanatical revolutionary bent on destroying the society in which he'd lived the first fifty or so years of his life, I never learned, though I did learn that he was just as I have described him: whereas AkweNema and the lord DessaTyso and the bulk of the members of the Brathel-Lanza desired only to simplify and reorder the caste system of NakrehVatee, to introduce into it more elements of justice and mobility between the castes, Kaph-No would have been truly satisfied with nothing less than the total abolition of the caste system itself. That was his desire. But he was an intelligent and realistic enough man to know that that was something he'd never see in his lifetime. He would have to settle for half of that loaf: the accomplishment of the stated goals of the BrathelLanza. But it galled him.

And, as a rule, he was a shy, reserved man, little given to talking in the presence of strangers, or even in the presence of close acquaintances unless it was concerning one of the many subjects of which he had mastery.

A high-level technologist by birth and training, KaphNo had never stopped his education, and could, at the drop of a suitable hat, argue medicine with AkweNema and ThefeRa, microbiology with SkorTho, psychology with GrelLo, or aesthetics with EnDera. And as often as not he would win those arguments.

Why he seemed to like me so well I had no idea— it was certainly not because I was his intellectual peer! —but I found myself flattered that he did. In turn, when I learned to take his frequently taciturn behavior with a grain of salt, I got to like him as well. Of all those in the Underground, he was the only man I really did like without reservation.

And I wasn't certain whether I really liked EnDera all that well. I felt a strong physical attraction for her, of course, and there were many things I did like about her personality, her mind, and I could understand her problems and even sympathize with them, but I'm not certain that I sympathized with her revolutionary ardor, though I'm sure her hatred of the system against which she fought was very similar to the hatred of the Kriths and all they stood for that had grown in me.

Yet—and this is the strange part—neither did I sympathize with KaphNo's even greater revolutionary ardor, and I called him friend.

"All the world's a bit queer, but for thee and me," said the old Pennsylvania Dutchman, "and sometimes I wonder about thee."

You know, there are times when I wonder a little even about myself. . . .

11

Of a Dream, and of Identities

When I had been in the Underground only a little over a month, my replicates had reached ML-2Y and looked very much as I must have looked as a two-year-old. Their lives differed in that they were never really conscious, and were taken from their encanters every other day for brief periods during which their muscles were exercised—cerebral programming had given them only the vaguest hint of what walking was all about. Then the replicates looked like 342 identical little brothers, normal and happy, if always "asleep."

In many ways it seemed much longer than a month to me, though I was certain that by now it must be about the first of October, as time was measured by the calendars of a world a long way from this Here and Now.

Two weeks later AkweNema's "daughter" was decanted for the last time and gradually awakened to the world outside the glass cylinders in which she'd grown from the cells taken from a dying girl's body. Education, in addition to the cerebral data fed to her before decanting, was begun, and every effort was made by the psychology team to re-create in the replicate a personality as similar as possible to that of the real daughter. AkweNema's reaction to the seeming resurrection was hard to gauge, but I got the impression that it alternated between delight and horror, and filled him with an almost morbid fascination he could not effectively fight. And there were times when KaphNo seemed to regret the growing of the replicate; things might have been easier for AkweNema had his daughter died once and for all.

At the same time as the replicate girl's decanting, my own replicates had reached the stage of three-year-olds and looked like a band of miniature HarkosNors—or Eric Matherses, the name to which I was more accustomed—or even Thimbron Parnassoses, as I had been called when I was their age, or rather at their "maturation level."

Like AkweNema, I didn't know whether I was fascinated and awed by the replication process or disgusted and frightened by it. Maybe it was a mixture of both, with a touch of narcissism thrown in for flavoring.

And as the time passed in the Underground, the dream I'd had a year before kept coming back to me:

A city of towering buildings and streets and parks illuminated in the night by floating globes of light, a city that I could see in my dreams but dimly and with double vision, poorly and out of focus and half hidden by rain and mist, but what I saw told me that it was no city I had ever seen before, no city ever built by humankind.

Despite the floating light globes, much of the alien city lay in darkness and shadow, and after a while, as my vision cleared, I saw movement in those shadows, furtive movement, stealthy and quiet, a figure here, another there, wrapped in dark clothing, but now and again betrayed by a glint of light from metal. All the moving figures in the quiet city carried weapons.

One of the dark-clad figures stepped briefly into light and for a moment I saw him clearly: a man in his thirties, tall and scarred from many battles, tanned, blond, wearing a short beard; he carried a Paratimer R-4 power pistol in his right hand, a knife in his left. This man, whom I shockingly recognized, turned as if facing me, as if peering into *my* eyes, and on his lips was a twisted, bitter smile of anger and hatred, of satisfaction and revenge. Then he turned away and vanished into shadows.

In another place another figure revealed itself momentarily. This too was a tall, scarred, blond, bearded man in his thirties, and he carried a large, heavy energy rifle in both hands.

And in still another place, stepping out of the shadows for a moment to make his way forward, was the same man. An army of men in the night, all identical, all perhaps cloned from a single person—so went my dream.

The army of raiders slipped silently through the night, all headed for a single destination wherein lay something they/he wished to destroy. In my dream there was a chill in me such as I'd never known before.

Time had gone by now, how much of it I didn't know, and they had almost reached their goal when, in the sky above the nonhuman city, a great light burst, white and brilliant, destroying the shadows and revealing those who had hidden in them. For a moment the raiders stopped in their tracks, startled by the light; then, as if guided by a single mind, they darted forward, running through the streets and across the park-like areas toward the largest building of the city.

From the building gunfire opened, sending shot and flame into the streets and the parks, and from the portals of the building issued an army of men—they, too, all identical, or nearly so—and all of them looked very much like a man—no, a *being* whom I'd known as Mager, a being who was slender and wiry and had a face made of craggy planes and tiny white lines like scars, who had neural organs complex enough to be called "brains" in addition to the one he had in his head. His type was very hard to kill. . . .

The Mager-force rushed into the streets, automatic slug throwers in their hands, spitting leaden death into the attackers, whose leading element was within range of the defenders' weapons. One of the blond men took a bullet in the chest. . . .

I staggered backward from the impact of the slug as it ripped through the right side of my chest just below the nipple, shattering ribs, puncturing a lung, exiting through my back, and tearing away great globs of flesh. I staggered backward more shocked than pained, stunned, dazed, knowing as the pain began that the wound was mortal and I was going to die.

I tried to raise my stolen R-4 power pistol, to take at least one of the Magers with me, but I didn't have the strength; the pistol was too heavy, slipped from my weakened grip, fell to the earth, and in moments I followed it, darkness, pain, and death coming over me as I fell.

The first of *me* died, but more of *me* came on, a dozen, two dozen; and here and there, as the collective *I* rushed forward, the individual *I* took more wounds. One of me was hit in the head, my skull shattered. I died instantly.

But I'd also taken a gut wound, a *me* some yards away, and I lay in agony as blood seeped onto the ground.

And I ran forward, a different *me,* a stream of bullets ripping away my left arm, but somehow I still fired with my right until I collapsed in unbearable pain.

Yet still, dying here and there, others of *me* terribly wounded, *I* came on against the Magers and still they killed me, though I wouldn't stop until they'd killed *me* all. . . .

And maybe they never would.

There my dream ended; it always ended there every time. And I wondered about it.

Oh, the Tromas in their wisdom had assured me that I had no psionic abilities, none at all, so I couldn't possibly be precognitive, could I? The dream couldn't possibly be some dim vision of the future, seen through a glass darkly, could it? Well, could it?

Religion didn't play a major role in the lives of the common people of NakrehVatee. It was there and was given lip service. The Bright Lords of Life and, more importantly, the Dark Lords of Death were given their due, but no more than that. Only among those of the higher castes, those who truly believed that through the cycles of reincarnation they had at last reached the point where they could hope to abandon the Wheel and look forward to an eternity in the land of the Blessed beyond the darkling waters of the Mountains of the West, was a great deal of thought given to the preparation and maintenance of the tombs in which their physical bodies would be preserved. Rather than a way of life, to most NakrehVatea religion was a mood, a coloring that seeped down to them from the higher reaches of the social pyramid, and really not much else.

And if most of the people of NakrehVatee had little regard for religion in their day-to-day lives, then the members of the BrathelLanza had even less. The revolutionary movement did not embrace atheism, didn't exactly reject the idea of godhood itself, but it did at least reject the polytheism tacitly accepted by the bulk of the nation's population. Monotheism was the order of the day among the avant-garde of the BrathelLanza and, like so many other people who have traveled the long road from pan- to poly- to monotheism, they looked toward the sun as the physical manifestation of their concept of the deity—a la the golden sun disk of Aton introduced to the world by Ikhnaton some thirty-three centuries ago.

For this reason the BrathelLanza, along with the rest of the NakrehVatea on the surface world above, did celebrate at least one religious holiday each year, that of the Return of the Sun King from the Dark Regions of Cold, the Deliverance of Helios from the Lords of Death, the winter solstice.

It was also an opportunity to throw one hell of a party.

So on the evening of the day that would be called December 20 on some calendars, all work in the city of VarKhohs and in the underground chambers of the BrathelLanza came to a halt; shops and offices above, labs and training areas below were all closed, and the membership of the Brotherhood of Life congregated in the Underground's largest room, that which contained the drill field, a great, brightly lighted cavern cut out of the living stone.

I won't go into what was eaten and drunk that night, or what followed in the darkened corridors and shadowy rooms. I'll only say that when the morning came there was many an aching head and many a guilty conscience.

To soothe those consciences, and in an effort to overcome those aching heads, most of those who were able to drag themselves out of bed went to a morning service that was a mixture of religious teachings, astrological mumbo-jumbo, ancestor worship and moral indoctrination.

Although I was one of those able, if barely, to drag myself out of bed, wondering where EnDera had spent the night, for it certainly hadn't been with me—those hours for me had gone by in the company of a dark young lady whom I later learned had not been born from a mother's womb but from an encanter flask, but she was warm flesh and blood for all that—I wasn't one of those who went to the services.

Rather, after a breakfast of coffee, raw eggs in milk and a brace of pills I hoped would make me feel halfway human again, I cleaned myself up, dressed in the military-type garments I'd begun to wear and went for a walk through the subterranean chambers.

My wandering footsteps unconsciously but purposefully took me through the strangely quiet and empty tunnels and passageways to the laboratories and finally into the large chamber where the 340 surviving replications of myself were still sleeping peacefully, totally unaware of the frenzy and gluttony that had passed through the chambers the night before.

For a long while I stood there looking at them, the replicates, the clones, the miniatures of me.

About two weeks before they had been transferred from the first of the maturation encanters to the second, where they would remain until they reached a maturation level of twelve years, which was still some two and a half months away. Now they were at ML-7Y, looking for all the world like sleeping little boys of seven years of age who would soon wake up and want to go outside and play ball or something.

And that mixture of awe and revulsion passed through me again, and once more I wondered about the wisdom—and the morality!—of this thing I'd gotten myself involved in.

So deep was I in these thoughts and feelings that I didn't hear the footsteps behind me until they had nearly reached me. When I did hear them I turned.

"Good morning, General," said OrDjina, the lovely mistress of the lord DessaTyso, with perhaps a slightly mocking tone in her voice as she spoke the last word, my title.

"Oh, good morning," I replied, wondering what had brought her here. To view her own replicate? I wondered, but remembered that the more mature clone of the cells of this woman was in another chamber, having some weeks before been encantered in a cylinder large enough for the final stages of her growth to maturity. So . . . ?

"You are not a religious man, I take it, General," she said, again with a mocking sound to the final word.

I shook my head and I looked her up and down in a fashion that I was sure was obvious to her, though she made no attempt to shrink from my gaze, to show a modesty I knew she didn't possess. More an exhibitionist than a shrinking violet, she.

Her clothing this morning was a tan outfit consisting of a thin, loose-fitting blouse with lace sleeves that ended at her elbows, the neckline of which plunged almost to her waist and under which she wore nothing, her full breasts straining to escape the capturing fabric. She wore equally loose-fitting trousers, which were cut with checkerboard squares down the outsides of her hips and legs and through which her dark skin showed from thigh to ankle, warm skin, inviting skin. The color of the clothing was slightly lighter than that skin, a shade that looked well with it.

Her black hair, brushed and gleaming, sparkling with a cluster of jewels above each temple, swept loosely across her shoulders and down her back. In her eyes was a sparkle that might have been mischievous had she had a greater air of innocence about her. But then, like modesty, innocence was a quality Lady OrDjina lacked. And she did not seem to regret that lack.

"And what about yourself?" I asked. "You don't feel a need for the sacred services?"

She laughed, flashing bright teeth. "I rather doubt it would do me any good. I am far beyond that point. Like yourself."

She turned to look into one of the glass cylinders that contained what appeared to be a naked seven-year-old boy. "You were a handsome child, General."

"I like to think so myself."

"And one who showed great promise for the man he would become," she said, and almost leered as she gestured toward the child's genitals. "And I rather imagine you were a nasty little boy as well."

"What do you mean by that?" I wasn't offended by either comment, only curious about the second.

"All little boys are nasty, you know. Some are just a bit more wicked than others."

"Do you really think so?"

"Of course."

"Well, maybe I was. At least my parents seemed to think so. I got more spankings than any other boy I knew."

She laughed. "You must have been a terror to the little girls when you grew a bit older."

I shrugged again.

Then she asked, something flintlike coming to her dark eyes, "And who were those parents you just spoke of, General?"

I turned to look her fully in the face. "Why do you ask that?"

"Curiosity. I would like to know a number of things about you."

"Such as?" What was she getting at?

"Oh, such as, where did you *really* grow up and what was your name then? Such as, what kind of a city or town did you live in and what was the language you spoke then?"

"You want to know a lot, don't you. Why?"

"Curiosity, as I told you." There was a pause, and the wicked gleam in her eyes sparkled brightly. "Because, General HarkosNor, I don't think there's a single word of truth in all those things you told psychologist GrelLo."

"Everything I told her was supposed to be kept confidential."

"Oh, General, it is being kept confidential, I can assure you. I haven't told a soul a thing I know about you—which, in truth, is absolutely nothing."

"But GrelLo let you go through my tapes and notes, is that it?" I should have been angry, but at the moment I was only worried. What was it that OrDjina suspected about me? The truth? Hardly that, I thought. I hoped.

"Honestly, General, do you think GrelLo could have prevented me even if she'd wanted to and tried?

I am the lady of his lordship, you know, and with his permission I can do just about anything I want."

"Just about?"

She sighed, placed a hand between her breasts, fingers touching the column of her neck. "I must admit that even his lordship finds it wise to defer to Akwe-Nema at times. For now," she added with an ominous weight.

"I see."

"Are you certain even of that, General?"

"Right now I'm not certain of much of anything."

" 'A wise man is one who admits his ignorance.' That's an old saying of my people. My people have a great number of old sayings." She paused long enough to look me up and down as I had looked her up and down a short while before. Then she spoke again: "I have been around a bit, General. NakrehVatee is not my home, as I'm certain you've surmised. My experiences have been, shall we say, a bit more cosmopolitan than those of most of the others here. And I know that you are not what you claim to be. General, your accent isn't even that of a SteeMehseeha, you know."

She raised a hand toward my face to keep me from speaking until she had finished. "I've been looking into your computer identity records, General, and I must say they are excellent forgeries. It would take an expert to find fault with them. But they're all lies, aren't they?"

"Does it make any difference what I say?"

"None whatsoever. Unless you wish to tell me the truth. But somehow I doubt that you'll do that."

"You're right there at least."

"Then should I go to AkweNema and KaphNo and tell them what I know? Should I ask them to do a little checking about you, more than they've already done?" She laughed a strange, almost bitter laugh. "Oh, those poor fools! You could be a government agent for all they know, come to infiltrate the BrathelLanza and bring all the power of the state down to crush them."

"I'm not that."

"I know."

"You're certain?"

"I'm certain of several things that you aren't, General. One of the things you aren't is a government agent. Another is a barbarian mercenary come across the sea to sell your fighting skill to the highest bidder. What I don't know is what you *are*."

"Then why don't you do like you said, tell Akwe-Nema and KaphNo and Lord DessaTyso what you know? Why didn't you do that before you even spoke to me?"

"Honestly, General, I have no desire to do that. I suspect certain things about you, things that I'm not even sure I can put into words. But I also suspect that you find it to your advantage to do exactly what the BrathelLanza expects of you. Whatever else you are, I don't think that you're about to betray them."

"You're right in that too."

"So I will not tell them."

"I'm still not certain I understand why."

"Your understanding is not necessary, General, only your knowledge that it is so."

"Okay. I guess."

She smiled that wicked smile again. "Just continue to do as they wish you to do, General. You and I are on the same side, you know, and it is to the advantage of us both to see that the BrathelLanza is successful. Isn't it?"

With that she turned, gazed briefly once more into the cylinder, at the naked little boy inside, then turned back to me again, a frank look coming to her eyes. "Wicked little boys can be a lot of fun."

Did I comprehend her meaning? I wasn't certain until her hands went to the clasps of her thin blouse, released them, and her breasts broke free of the fabric.

"We are quite alone," she said as she shrugged out of

the blouse. "I took the precaution of locking the doors when I entered."

"But . . ." I began to say, then thought better of it.

"You are interested? You would like to make love with me?" she asked as the blouse fluttered to the floor and her hands went to the belt of her trousers.

"I would be a liar if I said no."

"Then do not lie to me about that, General." She released the belt and then the clasps that held the trousers at her waist and allowed them to drop to the floor.

"Am I not as beautiful as you imagined?" she asked, smiling wickedly.

"More so," I said, feeling the stiffening within my own trousers, forgetting any fears I might have had of being discovered by the henchmen of the lord Dessa-Tyso. To hell with him.

"And let us see if you have fulfilled the promise the boys within the encanters show," she said, stepping toward me, reaching to loosen the clothing I wore.

"Oh, yes, General, you have fulfilled that promise," she said, flowing into my arms, her breasts crushing against my chest, her hands going to the throbbing point of passion I presented her.

"The floor here is not soft," she whispered as she went to her knees before me, "but it will do when the time comes for that. But first . . ."

Later, when she was gone and I was alone in the encanter chamber, silent except for the soft sounds of the machinery that supported the lives of the 340 replicates of myself, I wondered just what was the meaning of all the words she had spoken to me before the passionate, almost savage bout of sexual delight had begun.

My speculations could be endless and would probably be equally fruitless. How could I begin to understand a woman like her?

I shrugged and dressed and started back toward my suite, thinking that now my stomach might be able to take some solid food. With the lady OrDjina I had worked up quite an appetite, another appetite having been quite thoroughly satisfied.

12
Of OrDjina

In early January, as I logged the days in a private journal, OrDjina's replicate, finally given the name QueZina, was decanted and gradually brought to consciousness, as had the replicate of AkweNema's daughter before her. QueZina, looking like an unusually beautiful eighteen-year-old, was not to be given extracts of her senior's memory, but was to be allowed to develop her own personality through educational experiences not greatly unlike those of a normal human child, though starting from a psychological maturity much greater than that of a newborn and proceeding at a much more rapid pace. It was more on the order of an experiment than anything else, and one to which OrDjina and the lord DessaTyso had given their blessing.

I saw little of AkweNema's "daughter," who had been named AkweIetana. AkweNema spent more of his time on the surface than he did in the Underground, while the replicated girl remained below, usually in his suite, with nurses and teachers when she wasn't being given mnemonic instruction by GrelLo's people. The few times I did see her, during rare visits to Akwe-Nema's suite, left me with the impression of a very shy little girl inhabiting a big girl's body and totally uncertain of what to do with it. And each time I saw her, or OrDjina's replicate, QueZina, or one of the other half dozen or so adult replicates that lived in the BrathelLanza's Underground, I again felt those perplexing mixtures of feeling I had experienced before and that grew stronger with the passage of time. My attitudes toward replicates, even my own, never really did become clear to me.

In the early part of February, if my record keeping and calculations are at all accurate, my own replicates were placed in the last of the series of developmental encanters, the ones in which they would grow to maturity and from which they would go into a more or less normal kind of existence.

The boys, the 337 duplicates of myself at twelve years of age—another three had died; however, I was told, this was a surprisingly low rate of attrition—all had long blond hair upon their heads, silken like that of girls, and pubic hair, still little more than pale fuzz, had begun to grow around their genitals. Puberty was coming to them, and I wasn't at all certain that I was ready for that yet. Another 337 of *me* out running loose and leching after women. Mother, bar the door! Could the universe really stand that?

Meanwhile, the recording of my memories was progressing well, though it was a time-consuming operation, as KaphNo had warned me. In another month or six weeks, psychologist GrelLo assured me, the work would be all but completed and be ready for my editing, which should be accomplished rather quickly.

My training and education in other areas had been nearly completed by then, and I found myself with more free time than I'd had before, free time that I thought I should guard jealously, since once the replicates were finally decanted, I wasn't likely to have any time of my own. Day and night I would be preparing *them* for the target day of the revolution, which I figured to be about 1 September 1973.

The lady OrDjina hadn't spoken with me or approached me again, though I'd noticed her observing me at odd and unexpected times, and wondered just what in blazes she was up to. But then, could anyone answer that question for me?

As we looked through the index of tapes before the wall-filling holotank, EnDera asked, sounding as innocent as she could, "Is the lady OrDjina following you around?"

I looked up from the index display and said, trying to sound innocent too, "What do you mean?"

"Oh, nothing." Still little-girl innocent. "It's just that she keeps turning up at the oddest places, but only when you're there too."

"So you've noticed it."

"Uh-huh. Well, is she?"

"Following me? It looks that way."

"Why?"

I shrugged. "Damned if I know."

"I don't like it." Jealousy in her voice?

"It is a little disturbing sometimes."

"She must have a reason."

"Maybe she just likes me."

Jealousy in her face now. "She'd better keep her distance."

"Oh?"

She nodded. "If she's trying anything with you . . . well, if I don't get her, the lord DessaTyso will."

"The jealous type, is he?"

"Uh-huh. And he knows how to use that little gun he carries."

"Does he really go around armed?"

"Uh-huh. He's got a flat little pistol under his armpit. Nasty thing."

I just nodded. I wasn't surprised. And I thought I'd better watch myself if the lady OrDjina wanted to roll in the hay another time. Not that she wasn't a very delightful partner, but I didn't like the idea of being shot at by a jealous lover.

"And I'm the jealous type too, Harkos," EnDera was saying, as if perhaps she'd caught a glimpse of the memories of OrDjina that were passing through my mind.

"Yeah, I'm beginning to realize that." And maybe EnDera's relationship with me was now more than just an assignment from her superiors in the BrathelLanza. But then I'd suspected that for some time. "She's a strange one," I said aloud.

EnDera grunted affirmatively.

"She's not a NakrehVatea, is she?"

"No, she isn't. If I understood correctly, she's from somewhere in EkhoVro." That was the political entity that governed a portion of southern Europe and areas of northern Africa in this Here and Now. "I don't even think she's ever become a citizen." A smugness, a superiority in EnDera's voice? I wasn't certain.

"Then what's she doing in the BrathelLanza?" I asked. "I thought only native-born NakrehVatea were allowed into the inner circle—except for me, of course."

"She's here because of DessaTyso." She didn't give him his honorific, I noticed. Maybe she wasn't any too fond of his lordship. "She has been his mistress for some time now, I understand, but his family doesn't approve of her. They think he ought to have only native-born girls of his own caste sharing his bed. So there was something of a family brouhaha over her— and it wasn't even kept in the family: the Blues got wind of what was going on and let it leak to the public, mention was even made of it at the Council of Forty, which got DessaTyso's father, Lord DessaAnjoh, into hot water. The Reds supported DessaAnjoh in a vote of confidence in the council, but it put him in a bad spot for a while. The families of the members of the Council of Forty are supposed to be above reproach. Anyway, to smooth things over, DessaTyso let it be known that he was parting company with Lady OrDjina and pretended to send her away. Actually what he did was get AkweNema to consent to let her live down here, with a suite and all, and even a personal servant for her. He claimed she was always one of us in spirit anyway. And she seems satisfied enough—or so I thought. And I don't doubt that DessaTyso is."

"Must be a nice arrangement for him. This way he

can mix business and pleasure whenever he comes down."

EnDera nodded.

"What do you know about her background before she was his mistress?"

"Not too much. Mostly gossip, rumors, you know. The story is that she was some sort of *entertainer* in EkhoVro. Now, I wouldn't say exactly *what kind* of entertainer. Some say she was a singer or actress or something, but there are others who claim she did most of her work from flat on her back, and if she used her mouth it wasn't to sing or talk."

How right you are, I said to myself, but to EnDera I said, "I follow you. The same way she earns her keep now?"

"Exactly, only now it's with just one man and not a parade of them. Anyway, it seems that there was this government minister in EkhoVro she got mixed up with; they had a very wild, flashy affair or something. He left his wife and family and moved in with OrDjina in a pleasure-house where she was performing as a nude dancer and maybe staging some private sex shows with male dancers—and even a baboon, so one story said. Anyway, when word of this got out, there was a major scandal and a shake-up in the government. The minister was relieved of his position and OrDjina found it wiser to leave the country the first chance she got.

"And exactly how a person with her reputation ever got a visa to enter NakrehVatee, I'm not certain, but it may be that the lord DessaTyso"—when she pronounced his honorific this time it was with a touch of sarcasm—"already knew her then and pulled some strings to get her admitted. Anyway, that's what the Blue Chairman said, and that's why DessaTyso's father got in trouble. You just don't mess with immigration rules, you know."

"Still, it seems odd," I said. "I mean, allowing an

alien like her into the very heart of something that's supposed to be as secret as the BrathelLanza."

"You're an alien too, Harkos, at least technically."

"Well, I've got something the BrathelLanza needs— my skills."

"OrDjina's got something DessaTyso needs too—and it's right between her thighs."

"Okay. Okay."

"Not that I'm saying I approve," EnDera added quickly. "I can't say that I like her or trust her, and neither does Akwe. One of the rules he set up and made DessaTyso agree to was that she wouldn't be allowed to leave the Underground or communicate with another outsider prior to the revolution."

"That sounds wise."

"But I'm not certain Akwe can enforce it."

"Why's that?"

"If DessaTyso wants to smuggle her out some night when Akwe's not around, who's to stop him? KaphNo doesn't have the authority, and I think he's about the only one who'd even have the guts to try to stop him."

"I see what you mean." I paused, then asked: "Do you think there's any chance that she's an agent of some foreign power? EkhoVro or some other country?"

"The thought has crossed my mind. Why do you ask?"

"I don't know. There's just something, well, strange about her."

"That's what I've been trying to tell you, Harkos."

"So we're in agreement."

"As long as you don't try to get firsthand information about her background *or* her professional skills."

"Don't worry. I'd just as soon go to bed with a she-tiger."

"That would be just about as safe as touching her, I promise you."

"I accept the warning, and give you my promise that I'll stay clear of her." And maybe I really meant it.

EnDera laughed. "I wasn't really worried."

I glanced at the illuminated tape index and then back at EnDera. "Do you really want to look at a tape? I can think of a better way to pass the evening."

"Yes, I believe I can too," she said, a smile flickering across her lips as she began to open the loose gown she wore.

"Right here?" I asked as I reached for her, one hand entering the open gown and cupping a full breast.

"Right here would be fine," EnDera replied in hardly more than a whisper, her hands beginning to tug at my clothing. "Right here would be delightful."

13

The End of the BrathelLanza

On the morning of 4 March—of that date I am as certain as I am of any in my life: 4 March 1973—KaphNo joined me for breakfast. EnDera wasn't there. The day before, she had gone up to the surface to transact some business concerning the sale of her paintings and to collect some sums of money due her, and although she had been expected to return by the evening of that day, she still wasn't back the next morning.

I really wasn't too worried about her: EnDera was a grown woman, and she could take care of herself in the streets of VarKhohs perhaps better than I could have myself; but I was a little on edge because of her absence, and even more so when KaphNo, over coffee and rolls, told me that EnDera wasn't the only one who had failed to return from the upperworld during the past two days.

"Are you certain?" I asked him.

KaphNo nodded as he nibbled on a sweet roll, then said, "Day before yesterday two of my technicians went up to see about procuring some equipment for one of the labs—rheostats and such for electrical control units. They should have had no trouble obtaining them."

"But they didn't come back?"

KaphNo grunted. "I sent another technician up yesterday to find out what happened to them—they were young fellows, you know, and might have stopped for a drink and had a few too many. You know how it is. I wasn't worried. *Then* I wasn't worried."

"You are now?"

He grunted again, munched his roll, and swallowed

with the aid of coffee. "The one I sent up to check on them didn't come back either."

I shook my head. "Any idea what's going on?"

He shook his head in return. "None, but I did give Akwe a call last night, and he said he'd see that it was checked out from his end. I haven't heard from him yet. Maybe he'll call soon. I hope he does."

"And now EnDera," I said, mostly to myself.

"If I don't hear from Akwe soon, I'll punch him up again and have him get someone to check on her. Will that make you feel better?"

"I'll feel better when I know she's okay. Has anything like this ever happened before?"

KaphNo shook his head again, opened his mouth, popped in the remnants of the roll, and washed it down with more coffee. "Don't get too worried yet, Harkos. It may be nothing at all."

"And it may be something."

"Let's hope not," he said, and I remembered En-Dera's words: "Really, Harkos, we don't have too many illusions down here. We know we're under sentences of immediate execution on the spot, or prolonged torture in some of the lords' dungeons, if we're ever caught. We just hope we can put off being caught for a few more months."

"Cheer up, boy," KaphNo said as he refilled his coffee cup and reached across the table for another roll. "Your memory-recording sessions are just about over, aren't they?"

"Another two or three days. Then we'll start editing them."

"GrelLo and her people are going to have to start pushing their end of it. ThefeRa and SkorTho are anxious to start giving the replicates some preliminary tapes."

"It's a little early for that, isn't it?"

"Not for the most basic kinds of stuff, mainly muscular control, dexterity, that sort of thing. The boys are at ML-14Y, you know." There was in his voice a genuine affection for my replicates. "We could use some of the tapes we already have on this sort of thing, but we'd prefer to use yours from the start. It could save a lot of retraining later."

"So I've been told."

"And how are the other things going?"

"Well enough. I think I pretty well know my job now, and who the bad guys are."

KaphNo smiled. "And who the good guys are too?"

"They're the ones I wonder about sometimes."

"Anyone in particular?"

"Yes. The lord DessaTyso's playmate, the lady Or-Djina."

KaphNo gave me a serious look and nodded. "I know exactly what you mean. If it had been up to me, she would never have come down here in the first place."

"Do you think she could be a danger to us?"

KaphNo tilted his head to one side, pursed his lips. "I don't know," he said seriously. "I can't say that I entirely trust her, but she's never given me any reason to think that she might be, well, a danger to us. I mean, I've no reason to think she's a spy or a government agent or anything of that sort."

I could have said that maybe I did, but I didn't say that. If I were to tell him that much, then I'd have to tell him a lot of other things I didn't want him to know, like who and what I really was and why I was there.

"I guess I'm just worrying too much," I said finally.

"In a place and a situation like this one, we all worry too much, Harkos. And it's bad for the digestion." Then he sighed and forced a smile onto his face. "But it won't be much longer now. Two months or so more for the replicates to complete their maturation, and another two months or so to train them. In four months, five at the most, you'll be ready, your 'army' will be ready, we all will be ready. Then we'll show some people what a revolution is all about." The thought of coming violence, though it might not reach quite to the ends he desired, seemed to animate the old man, to quicken the blood in his tired veins and bring a fresh light to his deep-set eyes.

"I'm getting sort of anxious myself," I said.

KaphNo started to say something more, but was interrupted by the chiming of the kitchen communicator. Since he was closer to it, he reached up and punched the holotank to life, which quickly displayed the image of a young man whose name I didn't know, one of the security guards who, in AkweNema's absence, answered to KaphNo.

"Yes, what is it?" KaphNo asked.

"Master KaphNo, sire," the young guard began in an uncertain voice, "please excuse me for calling you at this hour, but, sire, I thought I'd better report it to you."

"Report what?" KaphNo asked, an edge of annoyance to his voice; he wasn't any too fond of his responsibility for security matters. "Spit it out, boy."

"The lady OrDjina, sire," the guard continued with the same hesitancy in his voice. "She is not in her quarters. Her servant says she has not been there since sometime yesterday."

"Are you certain?"

"Yes, sire. We are now in the process of searching the Underground—at the captain's orders, sire—but she does not appear to be anywhere about."

"Damn!" KaphNo muttered. "Well, continue the search, and inform your captain that I'll meet him in his office at once."

"Yes, sire. Very good, sire."

KaphNo turned off the communicator with an angry gesture, a frown wrinkling his face.

"What does that mean?" I asked.

"Damned if I know, Harkos," KaphNo said, suddenly looking very old again. "But, on top of everything else, I don't like the sound of it at all."

"Well, I . . ." I began, but was interrupted when the communicator buzzed again.

With another savage gesture KaphNo flipped the device back into operation. The image of GrelLo, the psychologist, developed in the tank this time.

"What is it, GrelLo?" KaphNo snapped.

"Is the general there?" she asked.

"I'm here."

"Oh, General," her voice said from the speaker, "have you forgotten? My technician is standing by for your recordings this morning."

"Oh, damn," I muttered. "I forgot the time." I glanced at KaphNo.

"Go on to the session," he replied. "Our security people can handle the other matter." He turned back to the holotank. "He'll be right there, GrelLo."

He switched off the device and turned to me: "Go on and get to the studio, Harkos. Those recordings are important too."

"Okay, but keep me posted, will you?"

"Yes, I'll certainly do that. As soon as I know what's going on."

KaphNo left the suite while I was dressing to go to the mnemonic-recording session. I never saw him again. I didn't know it then, of course, but I had already seen most of the members of the BrathelLanza for the last time.

Fifteen minutes later I was sitting in a large, comfortable chair with padded back and seat and supports for arms, legs, and head, while GrelLo's technician, a slender young man named MaLarba, was affixing electrodes to my scalp.

"Comfortable, General?" he asked. "You should be feeling the effects of the drugs soon."

Even as he spoke I could feel my body relaxing, seeming to begin to drift away from me, while at the same time my mind seemed to become sharper, clearer, more finely tuned, and the sensory data that came to me seemed more intense and more detailed, though soon I would lose consciousness of most of my senses, except for sight and hearing. I didn't particularly enjoy taking drugs that totally incapacitated me, that made me as limp and helpless as a newborn kitten, and then, on top of that, having myself strapped into a chair. I felt so vulnerable then. But that was one of the necessities of mnemonic recording, so I was told, and I went along with it. Two or three more sessions of it were all I would have to endure. I could stand that, couldn't I?

"That's the last of them," MaLarba said as he stepped away from the back of my head and came into my line of vision. "Now, if you'll allow me to strap you in." Not that there was much I could have done to stop him; I was now hardly aware of having arms and legs.

The technician passed the straps across my torso, arms, chest, hips, and legs, then tightened them down. I'd been told that the straps were purely for my own protection. I supposed it was so.

"All in place now, General. Let me know when you're ready to start."

My signal for that was a rapid batting of my eyelids; about the only things I had left that I could control volitionally were my eyelids and my eyes themselves.

Now I felt as if I were floating freely, a disembodied personality, only remotely connected to the outside world by eyes and ears.

I batted my eyelids.

"Very good, General," MaLarba said. He keyed the memory recorder; its buzzing indicated that the tapes were turning slowly above and behind me. "Now, yesterday, at the close of our session, General, we were . . .".

The passage of time while drugged was a very difficult thing to determine. I would drift off into memories and follow them through torturous paths and only after some time would I break out of my reverie long enough even to look out through my eyes. If I wished, there was a large chronometer on the far wall that I could see if I moved my eyes to the limit of their leftward motion. This time I didn't do that. Not yet.

I did open my eyes, however, and slipped back into a state of consciousness sufficient to comprehend what my eyes were seeing, my ears hearing.

Now MaLarba wasn't alone in the small recording room. A young female technician whose name I didn't know was standing facing him, twisting her hands together, a worried, even frightened expression on her face.

"I'm scared, really scared, MaLarba," she was saying.

"Maybe it's nothing. I'll go with you and we'll have a look."

"It might be better if we stayed here," the girl said.

"Now, GweZa, you're being silly. It can't be anything that bad. We'll go see."

The girl finally nodded agreement, but reluctantly.

MaLarba turned to glance at me, saw that my eyes were open, and stepped closer to speak to me. "General, there seems to be some kind of disturbance up front. I don't know what it is, but I'd better have a look. You'll be okay. We'll be right back."

I batted my eyelids in acknowledgment.

"Be right back, General," he said again, and went from the room with the girl.

With a mild but growing anxiety, I found that I couldn't go back inside and pick up my train of thought.

MaLarba would have to help me do that. When he came back . . .

A sudden fear struck me.

If he came back.

KaphNo's technicians hadn't come back, not the first two or the one he'd sent after them. And EnDera hadn't come back. And OrDjina was no longer in the Underground.

But, I told myself quickly, MaLarba isn't going to the surface, isn't leaving the Underground. He's just going a few yards up the tunnels.

It didn't help a bit. Something was wrong, I felt certain. And maybe getting a lot worse.

I turned my eyes as far to the left as they would go. The chronometer read 11:24:06. The digits that counted the seconds turned exceedingly slowly. At 11:24:57 I heard sounds, faint and remote, and at first I couldn't determine what was making them, chatterings that came and went like . . .

The sounds were louder, coming closer, and now I knew exactly what they were: automatic slug throwers, rifles and pistols both, chattering as conical slugs of metal erupted from their barrels. And I knew why EnDera and the three technicians hadn't come back from the surface. Why AkweNema had never returned KaphNo's call. They'd been arrested, maybe drugged, probably tortured, but definitely arrested. The day that EnDera and the others had dreaded, had hoped would never come, now had come.

The government finally was acting. The Brathel-Lanza was dying.

But what of OrDjina? How did her absence figure into this? . . . unless she had known, had perhaps even assisted the government. But I didn't think so. Then what? No answers. No more time to ask the questions.

Running feet outside the door. Hoarse calls and cries. A gagged scream. The sound of something heavy striking the floor. The terribly loud sounds of automatic weapons coming still closer.

More feet in the hallway outside the room, stumbling. A thud that rattled the wall beside the door, then a scratching on the door itself. The door opening slowly as if pushed by a small, curious but timid child. Someone entering, someone whom at first I didn't recognize; his face was a bloody wreck, part of his cheek blown away, white bone and shattered teeth exposed. Two ragged holes in the starched, white blouse of a technician, holes surrounded by a red wetness that spread even as he staggered toward me, then turned back, stumbled to the door, shut it, latched it, locked it. Then again toward me.

A distorted voice that bubbled with blood: "Police. General. Police. Come. To. Kill. Us. Kill. Us. All . . ."

What was left of MaLarba staggered forward another step or two, tried to get something else out, but the blood was too thick in his throat and he could not speak. He almost fell, then caught himself and grabbed the arm of my chair, wiping blood across it and across my hand. He bent, tried to reach for the buckles of the straps that held me in the chair, and touched one of them but was unable to loosen it.

Try, dammit, try! I yelled silently within my head.

He tried, yes, dammit, he tried to get me loose, but it was too late, he was already too nearly dead.

His knees gave way under him and he dropped to the floor, turning and rolling over as he did so that finally he lay halfway crumpled on his back. He turned his ruined face toward me, trying to say something with his eyes, but couldn't. He gagged on the blood, coughed, died. I hoped the Dark Lords beyond the Mountains of the West would receive him kindly.

I sat in the chair, unable to make the slightest move, filled with horror and fear. My friends, my allies, were out there dying, and their warrior, their battle leader, was helpless and was likely to die very soon himself.

Shadowy Man, I screamed inside my head, goddamn you, Shadowy Man, what have you done to me now?

There was no answer. I had expected none.

Outside the room, automatic weapons chattered still, though more randomly; hoarse calls still filled the air, orders, commands, a scream of pain, a cry for help, more explosive chattering.

My eyes went leftward. The digits of the chronometer said it was 11:29:44. Only five minutes?

More feet, more orders, more chattering of weapons, which had now almost come to a stop.

It was 11:32:07. Two pairs of feet outside the doorway. One stopping. Then the other, stopping, returning.

"What's this?" a voice asked,

"Probably just a storeroom or something. Let's go. We're just about finished."

"Sure about that?"

The thud of a booted foot kicking the door.

Now they'd find me. I was dead. Damn you, Shadowy Man!

"I said leave it," an authoritative voice said. "We got our orders. We got all the live ones and now we go back to the surface. Then we seal the place off and turn it over to the inspectors."

"It won't be very nice for them when they get around to it, if they're as slow as they usually are."

"That ain't our worry. Let them wait a couple of weeks if they want to. That's their tough luck if this places stinks like a slaughterhouse when they get here. Come on. Let's go. We'd better give NaTyso a hand with those prisoners."

"Yeah. Will do." A pause. "But, you know, it beats me why we couldn't have used gas down here. Would have been a whole lot easier and not nearly so messy."

"Hell, man, you know as well as I do that there's two ways to do anything: the right way and the official way. Let's go."

Feet moving away now, away from the doorway.

Soon other feet, shuffling leadenly across the floor outside the door. A woman sobbing. A man's voice saying: "Don't take it so hard, lady. You didn't get shot, did you? And neither did the girl." Woman sobbing louder. "And they might not even execute you. Life in a public brothel's not all that bad, so they tell me."

"What's—what's that?" asks a voice that might be that of a child, but isn't; it is the voice of the replicate of AkweNema's daughter.

"Don't you worry none, baby," the man's voice says. "It ain't no public whorehouse for you. Captain says he's gonna take you home for himself."

Girl and woman sobbing together.

Feet shuffling off into the distance.

Now 11:40:35. There is no sound in the Underground, save for the *shush-shush-shush* of air circulating through the vents somewhere above me, the buzzing of the recorder as it still operates, the hiss of tape across the recording heads.

Now I almost wished they had shot me. If I couldn't get out of the straps when the drugs wore off—and I was very much afraid that I couldn't; the straps were well made and MaLarba had done a good job fastening them—if I couldn't get out, then I might well die of thirst before the inspectors came to investigate the place, if the policemen I'd heard knew what they were talking about, and I was afraid they might. I might die of thirst, but I stood a pretty good chance of going out of my mind first.

I looked up as high as I could toward the ceiling, up toward the surface world so far away, and again I said to myself, Damn you, Shadowy Man, damn you to the deepest hell. . . .

14

Opening Corridors

I looked again at the chronometer—12:04:56—then down at the bloody, quiet, lifeless thing on the floor beside me, its sightless eyes turned toward the lighting strip that ran across the ceiling, as if during their final moments of vision they had sought the comfort of that glow. Forty minutes before it had been a human being, a technician, a young man named MaLarba; maybe his girl friend, GweZa, was dead too. Maybe KaphNo and ThefeRa and SkorTho and GrelLo and all the others were dead as well. And EnDera and AkweNema and perhaps even the lord DessaTyso were prisoners of the police and the state, if they weren't dead.

Once again I found myself alone, my friends dead around me, but there was a difference this time. I might be joining them soon. A few days at the most. I did not think my chances of getting out of that chair to be very good at all, and it would be some time yet before the drugs wore off enough for me even to make a probably futile attempt. So . . .

I wouldn't say that I became unhinged then, but for a while my grasp on reality slackened, a reality I could contact now only with my eyes and ears; and my eyes could see little, a narrow cone of vision; my ears could hear even less. For a moment I stood on the brink of something I couldn't grasp, couldn't understand, and then with an angry, silent scream, a curse thrown toward all the gods of all the Earths and toward the Shadowy Man, a curse that was mingled with a plea for help from those same malevolent forces, I plunged downward, inward, toward blackness, darkness, insanity, fear, terror . . . and fell all the way through and outward again, rushing upward, expanding into vast and empty corridors, chambers, halls. . . .

Of this I can speak only in analogies, for there are no words for what I experienced, not in any language I have ever known. If anyone has ever experienced this before, and if he has found a way of expressing it, I wish I could learn the way from him. As it was, no words. But it was *something* like this:

I had fallen into the darkness, screaming for help, and in some unconscious, unknowing way, that call had been answered, not by gods or by the Shadowy Man but by my replicates, my clones; through resonance they knew that I had asked something of them, though they did not know what, and they answered the only way they could: they opened themselves for me.

For the first seconds—read *years,* read *centuries*—I plunged, twisted, tumbled, turned, flew, soared. Out of the dark and fear-filled corridors of my own brain, I—whatever it is that is *I,* is *me*—swept into 337 sparkling new places, empty, virginal, untouched, waiting to be inhabited, waiting to be filled with sight and sound, with experience and memory.

I recoiled, drew back into the dark caverns of my own skull, found them not so dark now, not so frightening, yet crowded full, filled with memories aching to be freed, with thoughts waiting to be thought, dreams to be dreamed, fantasies to be conjured up, nightmares to be screamed at. They all wanted out—and now, for the first time in my life, maybe for the first time in anyone's life, there was a place for them to go, many places to go.

I reached out cautiously, gently, trying to narrow the mental probe I extended, trying to use the theories taught me by KaphNo and SkorTho and GrelLo, tried to exercise response control and select a single brain of a single replicate. Somehow, I did it.

On one level I knew, saw, felt, and sensed the organic brain of the replicate, the cerebral matter that provides the matrix from which the mind is built—from which a mind could be built, for as yet there had not evolved a mind from this raw cerebral material. This replicate had been deprived of all sensory data except on the lowest, most basic levels. The soil was fertile, rich, but no seeds had yet been planted.

On another level: again, vast and empty corridors, halls and chambers of potential consciousness, potential awareness. Corridors crying to be filled, begging for my entry, as if my slightest touch had made them aware, if but barely, of the vast and remarkable world outside.

I did not commit my next act volitionally. Perhaps if I'd wanted to I couldn't have accomplished it intentionally. But what happened, happened. . . .

My eyelids opened and I peered out of the murky liquid in which I half floated, felt the flow of it around my naked flesh, tasted the strange, comforting flavor of it in my mouth and took oxygen from it as I breathed it in through my lungs, heard it carry into my ears the sounds of the machines that kept me alive and growing.

Yet at the same time my eyes—my *other* eyes—looked around the recording room, saw the motionless corpse that had been MaLarba, saw out of their corners that the chronometer read only 12:05:02. Six seconds? And heard low rumblings that could have been only the swish of the air from the overhead vents and the slowed buzzing of the mnemonic recorder. It was something like being in X5 augmentation, but now the world was slowed by a factor much greater than five, slowed by powers of ten, by exponential factors.

And beyond either set of scanty sensory data, through the crowded corridors of my own brain and the empty ones of the replicates, I felt . . . I felt . . . Even analogies fail me here. As if I had expanded?

As if I had grown to twice my size? As if a portion of godhood had touched me and become a part of me? Or as if I had become a portion of the godhood?

I did expand—I am sure of that, if of nothing else. And out of the dim, dark rooms of my brain, out of the attics and cellars and closets of forgetfulness and of never having known, memory and unformed thoughts leaped free, dreams and visions jumped and gamboled across the connections, the junctions, the nexuses, spilling over, dancing free, running with the winds of a new freedom through fresh neural impulses.

For a thousand years I basked and shivered alternately in all the experiences of my life, seeing everything I'd ever seen before, everything I'd ever heard, ever felt, ever thought . . . yet with a clarity and a detail of vision I'd never before experienced or even imagined possible.

If not the fringes of godhood, then something terribly close to it.

I felt more fully realized than a human being has ever felt before.

But this was only one of them, only one of the replicates. And there were over 330 more of them. . . .

After another thousand years of reviewing only the most pleasurable of my life's experiences, I reached out again, probed with a more careful, wiser, more experienced touch. And there was another of the virginal brains, potential minds, more bright and empty corridors, and all waiting for me. I spilled into those empty places.

I had the same sensations as before, but this time I could experience them more critically, know them more intimately, all the beauty and ugliness, all the pain and pleasure. And again there were those feelings of expansion, of power. Again there were sensations of new, empty expanses of consciousness opening up before me, to be filled as fully as possible from the wells of my memory.

Now I was three. Not exactly HarkosNor/Eric Mathers anymore, but perhaps something bigger, better than he had ever been, something with at least the potential of being wiser, more intelligent, more able to grasp and understand the vastness of the worlds of my past experience.

I resonated between my own body and the bodies of the two replicates. Awaiting me were 335 more brains, more possible minds.

I reached out again.

And again.

And again . . .

15

Genesis

All I have now is my own memory, a memory confined and shackled by my very finite limitations. I am only one man now, as I record these things out of the past, and I can speak of them only as remembrances of once having been a part of that creation, a part of that existence, a part of that being who came into the universe when my mind and the personalityless minds of the replicates resonated together, operated as a single, thinking entity.

I am not that amalgam. But I was once a part of it.

And since I am not what *it* was, I cannot continue to use the first-person singular. I, Eric Mathers, will speak of it, of *him,* what I can still recall of him and of that existence.

All but one of the replicates were now joined in psionic resonance with the entity that had been their senior—*had been,* for now they were one, with 337 bodies, one of them drugged, strapped into a chair, the others still half floating in the solutions that filled their encanters. They comprised a single mind that was then the mind of Eric Mathers; during those first few moments, at least, it was the mind of Eric Mathers, for all his memories, his experiences, his opinions, and his beliefs had not yet changed; it was merely that there were more vessels to carry him, and like a gas under high pressure he had expanded to fill them, although in that very process he had begun to become something other than what he had been, something that no man had ever been before.

Of the 337 replicates, all but one were now component parts of this new yet nameless entity. One of the replicates, the victim of previously undiscovered brain damage, was incapable of entering into the union, was little more than a vegetable whose autonomic nervous system kept his body alive, but who had virtually no capacity for cerebral growth, for consciousness, for thought. That body was left alone, to continue its maturation as best it could.

The others that were now one: After aeons of wonder and visions, he paused for what seemed to him to be still more aeons, though now he had lost all contact with the outside material world and had no real means of reckoning the passage of external time, if the passage of time had any real meaning for him then, of which he was not yet certain. Time was something about which he would speculate, he told himself. There was much he could learn about the nature of time, much to be drawn from the experiences of the past, things Eric Mathers had seen and heard and read and done that related to the nature of time itself. He decided he would do that, determine the nature of time. But not just yet. There was no hurry.

He rested then, gathered his strength, composed mental forces the immensity and nature of which he had hardly begun to comprehend. He pondered that strength and found himself almost frightened by it. In a sense, he thought, the doors of the universe might be open to him. Some of the doors at least. But not all of them, perhaps.

He remembered, in clarity and detail he still found startling:

Back across time and space, to a Timeline called KHL-000 in the month of February, over a year before . . . The Palace of the Tromas. The Place wherein Dwell the All-Wise Mothers.

And of the Tromas themselves: female Kriths, a

dozen of them, ancient, deformed, scarcely hominid in their obesity.

In the air about them was an almost electrical aura, a sensation of power held in tight check, of vast forces unseeable and perhaps unknowable, psionic powers that the Tromas and their ancestors had utilized to build the power of the Krithian race, to allow them to expand across the Timelines, to bend even time itself to their uses.

Now he recognized the Tromas for what they were. In some ways he was very much like them. But he had many more bodies, many more brains than their dozen —but they had centuries of experience and accumulated skill behind them. How great were the similarities? How great the differences?

As with the questions he had raised about time itself, he left these questions about the Tromas hanging, filed away in a place from which they could easily be retrieved when the time came to fully investigate.

Now, like the playful child he was, the composite mind of the man and his replicates began to search again, to explore, to probe outside itself, to see what it could find outside the complex universe it was building for itself in the resonance patterns that existed between its members.

He probed outward this time, not inward, out into the vast gulf of psionic darkness, out into an empty universe lighted only here and there by remote brilliances, galaxies far away in the darkness of that emptiness, quasars on the very limits of observation.

He reached out across the expanses . . . and touched another mind.

He recoiled for a moment, held back, for he was not certain whether he wanted to enter this mind, whether he could if he wanted to, whether the resonance patterns there coincided enough for there to be the full response control of level three. He paused, held, pondered, decided: response-level two would be sufficient, might be the best he could do no matter how hard he tried. He moved forward, looked. . . .

*Lieutenant Colonel Eric Mathers sat on a bunk, a cigarette between his lips, an energy pistol disassembled in his lap. He was the only person in the room.

*For furniture there was the bunk he sat on, another, similar bunk, a desk between them, a battered old dresser opposite the desk, on the dresser a pile of soiled clothing. Beside the dresser was a lavatory, above the lavatory a shelf on which sat two sets of shaving gear, folded towels, a cracked mirror.

*As he slowly put the weapon back together, apparently bored with the operation, apparently finding it merely something to do while he waited, Lieutenant Colonel Mathers could hear from outside the room, from outside the small, frame building, the passage of motorized vehicles on a dirt road, the rumbling of laboring engines, the complaining of metal, the yells and curses of tired men.

*Then there was a knock on the door. Mathers looked up, said, "Yes?"

*The door opened just enough to allow the head of a young soldier to slip through. His mouth said, "Colonel, he's on his way here now. The Krith, sir." The language the young soldier spoke was Timeliners' Shangalis.

*"Very good, Corporal. Thanks."

*"Right, sir."

*The head retreated; the door closed.

*Lieutenant Colonel Mathers completed reassembling the energy pistol, snapped its power cartridge into place, slipped the weapon into the holster on his hip, rose to his feet, brushed off his clothing, and stuffed his shirttails into his pants. After taking a quick glance around the room, he snuffed out his cigarette and went toward the door.

*He opened it just in time to see a naked, ugly,

brownish, alien Krith come around the back of the jeep in which he had arrived, his brown-marble eyes bright, his long tail swinging in the air like an interrogation point.

*"Eric, my friend," the Krith said.

*"Mar-masco," Mathers said in reply, bowing in Krithian fashion as the alien did the same. "Come in," Mathers said, gesturing toward the doorway behind him.

*The Krith nodded and followed him.

*Mathers had seen the brown folder in his hand. The Krith had brought what Mathers was hoping he would bring.

*Inside, Mar-masco sat down on one of the beds, Mathers on the other.

*"I have brought exactly what you wanted of me, Eric."

*"Exactly?" Mathers asked.

*"Exactly," the Krith repeated, opening the folder and then spreading sheets of paper out on the rough woolen blanket on the bed. "The new contract confirms your rank and pay scale and bonus, all in order. I have a check here too."

*"Very good."

"You will be granted a month's leave on one of the Rajaian Lines, as you requested, expenses paid— that part took some doing, I grant you, but we felt that your services to the Timeliners warranted it. Your next assignment, when your leave is up, will be to . . ."

He withdrew, pulled back into the psionic darkness, reviewed things for a moment.

That was *me,* he thought, a version of Eric Mathers, a parallel Eric Mathers . . . still working for the Kriths as a Timeliner mercenary, as *I* once did, still loyal to them, still unquestioning of them, still waging their wars for them and helping them alter the histories of the parallel Earths so that they would fit into whatever master plan it was the Kriths had for the universe.

There were other stars in the darkness; he sought out one of them, found . . .

*Pain and darkness, one eye seeing dimly the walls of the hospital room to which he was confined. Eric Mathers tried to stir on his bed, tried to use the stump of an arm to relieve the pressure on the sores on his back, caused himself only more pain, fell back, groaned, tried to remember what it was like when he had been a whole man, when every moment was not one of agony, but found that he could not.

With that same grotesque stump, he fumbled, pushed a button that rang a remote bell, sent current pulsing through a distant, incandescent bulb. A nurse would hear the bell, see the light, and eventually would come to see what he wanted. A bedpan? A bath? A drink of water? And then he would try to tell her, try to make her understand, for the nurse on duty now was one of the new ones and had not yet learned to decipher the gagged sounds that passed for speech, the noises that came from the twisted throat of Eric Mathers, ex-Timeliner, hopelessly injured beyond repair, another casualty of the endless wars across the Lines of Time. . . .

Again he withdrew into the darkness of psionic space, shuddering within the resonance patterns of himself. The horror had been too great; he was not ready for *that* yet, for he knew exactly what *it* was . . . himself, a parallel version of Eric Mathers, so seriously injured in the explosion that had wrecked a place called Staunton on Line RTGB-307, where *he* had discovered the presence of a second alien race moving across the Timelines, altering worlds to suit *their* purposes, that he was now little more than a basket case, a painful distortion of a man confined to a hospital bed for the rest of his life. Mercifully, it would be a short one.

He rallied himself, collected the various components of himself, looked across the darkness once more at other points of psionic light, hesitant at first about approaching another, finally doing so, reaching out, probing, seeing. . . .

This was not quite as bad as the last one, though bad enough. . . .

*A tall blond man who appeared to be in his sixties, but who was actually less than forty years old, his face covered with a full beard, his emaciated frame covered with filthy prison garments, huddled in his gray stone cell, chewing a crust of bread, gazing up at the narrow window above his head, which was the cell's only source of light. A bright beam of sunlight passed through the window, illuminating motes of dust in the air, splashing a narrow rectangle of light, bright and yellow, against the far wall, obscuring the wall's many scribblings, executed over the years with bits of charred wood.

*The man in the cell was named Thimbron Parnassos; that was the only name he had ever known in his life. He had never been approached by the Timeliners, had never joined them, had never moved across the Lines of Time, waging the wars of the Kriths to change tomorrow, had never been given the name Eric Mathers during an assignment in an English-speaking country on a Line labeled by the Kriths RTGB-307.

*Parnassos continued to stare at the beam of sunlight, wondering what the world was like outside the prison now, for it had been more years than he could remember since he had seen anything outside the four gray walls that enclosed him. He did not think of it now, but the memory was always there, just below the surface, the memory of the last time he had seen the outside world: it had been a gallows yard, where he and a dozen other students waited for their turns to come, their turns to mount the steps and place their heads within the sweat-stained nooses, for the traps to be opened under them and for their bodies to fall, for their necks to be snapped as the ropes burned into their flesh. They had been convicted of sedition and treason against the government of North Ionia, and they were to die. But they did not die. A cruel quirk of fate. In celebration of a major victory over the rebellious forces, the governor of North Ionia had commuted their sentences to life imprisonment, solitary confinement, no chance of parole. Death would have been preferable. The boys were taken back into the gray prison, never to see the outside world again.

Parnassos rocked on his knees on the floor of the cell, his crust of bread eaten, his stomach still empty. He rocked on his knees and hummed to himself an old, old song his father had taught him as a child. His father had been very lucky. He had been hanged. But he didn't think of that very often either. He didn't think of very much at all. . . .

He withdrew in pain and confusion. He found it hard to believe that the huddled figure was himself, was Eric Mathers, another parallel of the man he had been. But it was. It was.

Across the darkness again, seeking still another pinpoint of luminance, another fragment of consciousness in the emptiness.

Touching. Contacting . . .

*The big blond man was dressed conservatively, his clothing unsuited for his frame, the cravat around his neck loosened. Under his coat and his shirt, his shoulders slumped and his back bent; it was as if he were trying to diminish his size, to appear smaller than he actually was, as if he did not wish to bring attention to himself, which was true.

*He stood behind a lectern, this man named Thimbron Parnassos, and behind him was a large map of North Ionia, labeled in Greek characters. Before him was a room filled with students, and he was lecturing to them in a variant of the Greek language about the period of troubles in North Ionia, the time, nearly two decades before, when a handful of anarchists and misguided students had risen in revolt against the lawfully established government, and how the government had ruthlessly but righteously put down the revolt, how all sedition in North Ionia had been done away with, and how the governor, in his wisdom, had established what Professor Parnassos could not call a "police state" but which was exactly that.

*Thimbron Parnassos, professor of post-Hellenic history, did not mention the fact that his own father had been among those rebels. Of course, all that was in the files of the Astefee—the secret police—and had caused him many an uneasy moment. But, of course, the police knew that he, Professor Parnassos, was a loyal subject of the state, had rejected his father, had denied any allegiance to the older man's involvement in rebellion, and even had been instrumental in helping to arrest the group of which his father had been a member. Over the years since adolescence he had proved himself loyal, dependable, and trustworthy, never one to say a word out of line.

But still he had nightmares sometimes, and there was a portion of himself he could not trust. One day, he knew, that mad side of himself would break free, would reveal itself, and then the Astefee would come for him. . . .

Repelled, he withdrew, pulled back into darkness.

Were they all like this? All the versions of Eric Mathers/Thimbron Parnassos? Were all the rest of *him* traitors?

Farther and farther back he pulled, across the darkness, across the Timelines, back toward the Earth of the BrathelLanza and the Underground and the laboratories that held the forms of Eric Mathers and his

336 replicates that were the source of the response patterns that were himself.

And as he came back and drifted into the corporeal bodies, he thought he was beginning to understand exactly what the Shadowy Man really was. Who he was. And what he had to do.

16

A Shadow Visits

Through 674 now-opened eyes he saw 337 different scenes. One of them was a mnemonic-recording chamber, brightly lighted, in which lay the body of a dead technician named MaLarba and the living form of Eric Mathers, still strapped into a reclining chair, the body still incapacitated by drugs. The other 336 views were essentially the same: looking out through murky fluids that were in constant motion before the eyes, looking out of the transparent encanter cylinders, across a space, an aisle, to another cylinder in which floated the naked form of a young boy, perhaps fourteen years of age, whose eyes were now open, who looked out of his own cylinder into his own eyes, and in the eyes that looked and in the eyes that looked back was a strange, uncertain, excited, and very curious consciousness.

Carefully now he forced 672 eyelids to close, shutting off the nearly identical scenes they saw. Finally he saw only one scene. That of the recording room. He commanded the single pair of eyes through which he looked to move. Reluctantly they did.

Nothing appeared to have changed in the room. It was exactly as he remembered it. There was no indication that the drug had worn off the body that called itself Eric Mathers. Nor was there indication that corruption had begun to dissolve the body that had been MaLarba. Yet it seemed that days, even weeks, had gone by. There should have been signs of *something*. Time could not have stopped. Could it?

Leftward the eyes moved, seeking the chronometer and the digits in its face that displayed the passage of time. The eyes stopped, and the composite mind of the senior and his replicates considered the data.

The chronometer read 12:09.31.

Five minutes. Less than five minutes. How was it possible?

Or had a full twenty-four or a full forty-eight hours passed?

No, that was not possible.

Although it seemed that he had been roving through paratime for days, for weeks, and before that more days or weeks integrating himself, it had been less than five minutes since he had come in contact with the first of the replicates and begun his expansion, his creation.

Only minutes . . .

Or was it that his composite mind now had command of chronological time as well as parallel time, of vertical time as well as horizontal time? Had he actually spent days—or years—in his own creation and in his quest, and then returned from out of time to place his consciousness in this particular present, less than five minutes after his beginning? Or did he perhaps exist in a unique sort of chronological time, a subtime, so to speak, which progressed toward the future in a linear fashion, but at a different rate?

Could these things be so? And if so . . .

The Shadowy Man could command time. The Tromas had said so.

And I . . .

For a while he rested, in real time, feeling the breathing of the body of Eric Mathers, hearing the *swish-swish-swish* of air circulating through the room, the hiss of tape across recording heads above and behind him, seeing the digits that represented seconds clicking one after another across the chronometer's face.

When the chronometer read 12:11:17 he began to withdraw from the body, to fully reintegrate himself, to divorce himself from all the corporeal bodies. He was going to try an experiment.

There were now within his mind vague bits and pieces of data, odd and long-forgotten remembrances, sensations he had collected during the time of his own existence as the composite mind. He thought he knew what to do, how to do it, but he was yet uncertain— and there is no way I can put into words these feelings and hunches he felt then. Again: there are no words in any language; it is an experience beyond the finite concepts of finite beings. But he did it.

Into the psionic darkness again, searching, seeking, finding . . .

A bright point of awareness, of consciousness, similar to the others he had encountered, yet also different, far more familiar than they had been, a stronger sense of kinship. Here was another Eric Mathers, another Eric Mathers there in the Underground, a conscious, living, breathing Eric Mathers who was terribly similar to the Eric Mathers who was now a part of the composite resonance pattern.

He did not actually *touch* that mind. That was not his plan, to enter into a second- or third-level resonance. He was going to try to do something else, something wild, fantastic—impossible, perhaps; yet, if *he could* do it . . .

Focusing all his attention on that spot of light that was the consciousness of *an* Eric Mathers, he began to formulate within himself the position of that spot of light in time and in space, at least four frameworks of reference, at least four sets of coordinates: and he saw that it was a roving, wandering, three-dimensional tube of light passing through space/time from a direction that could be labeled past toward a direction that could be labeled future. He narrowed his references. Selected a space/time. Again he focused his attention, isolated one particular fragment of space/time, and propelled himself toward it.

Frozen time. Frozen space. A universe stopped dead in its tracks. Almost. Now he could do it.

In spatial frameworks he selected a spot a few feet from where the consciousness was located. He moved toward that position, into it, projecting *something* of himself into the particular tiny fragment of all continuua, all-space, all-time. He focused and focused again, grasping molecules of air, photons of light, adjusting them, bending them, twisting them, altering them, making out of them something that had not been there before. Not a significant thing, perhaps. No great alteration of the matter/energy of that place/time. But enough.

Some portion of himself was in the same room with the other consciousness. He could now see, or do something akin to seeing, and he sensed a series of overlapping images broken from bits of the high end of the electromagnetic spectrum: an infrared image here, a yellow one there, an ultraviolet one at another place. And he sensed the twisting of the fabric of the universe, minor though it was, and the aura of power, the crackling of something not unlike electrical tension that filled the small concrete room. And he was aware of how *he,* this force he projected, would appear to the room's physical occupant: hazy, smoky, wraithlike, a shadowy form with the figure of a man, no more than that.

And he saw this: A small room with damp concrete walls; moisture; a dimly glowing strip of light ran across the ceiling; a cot was the only article of furniture in the room; Eric Mathers, *aka* HarkosNor, dressed in a robe that was an appropriate costume for the city of VarKhohs of NakrehVatee, sat on the cot, a pained expression on his face, a lump on the back of his head; the medicine given him by RyoNa had begun to do its work, but all the pain was not yet gone.

The *presence* he had created out of light and air waited for Mathers to become aware of it, of him.

Then Mathers *was* aware of the forces at play within

the room; he looked up toward the center point of those forces and saw the shape forming in the air.

There was silence in the room for long, dragging moments. He knew that Mathers was waiting for him to speak. He would do so; he thought he knew how. Grasping molecules of air, he took them in hand and set them to vibrating, to pulsing at carefully determined frequencies and amplitudes, to forming waves in the air that passed from his focal point toward that of Mathers. Yes, this seemed to be the right way. The sounds he created were: "Well, Eric, I hope you're not feeling too badly now."

The Eric Mathers who sat in the room and awaited the coming of RyoNa's "very important people" looked a little puzzled but not totally surprised. "I'm okay," he said at last. "I was afraid the Tromas had destroyed you back in KHL-000."

He could not suppress his feelings. That was *his* future of which Mathers spoke, something he was yet to encounter. But to Mathers, *this* Eric Mathers, it was something that had occurred some months in the past. Involuntarily he chuckled; the air carried his chuckle in waves across the room. How could he ever explain this to Mathers? "Damn," he made the air say more expertly, focusing the sounds across the room, sounds identical with those the vocal cords and mouth and lips and tongue of Eric Mathers would have made, "this could get confusing."

"What do you mean?" Mathers asked, still puzzled.

"What you're talking about is in your past, you see," he made the air say, "but it's in *my* future. It hasn't happened to *me* yet, so I don't know the outcome of our fight with the Krithian ladies any more than you do." He wanted to tell Mathers a great deal more, but he knew he dared not.

"I see," Mathers said.

"I hope you do, though I'm not positive I do. As I said, it *could* get confusing." It already was, but perhaps he was beginning to understand more and more of it.

"Yeah." Mathers grunted, that was all he did in way of reply.

He created sounds again: "Your head's not hurting now, and don't worry, you don't have a concussion. The lump will go away in a few days."

"That's comforting," Mathers replied grudgingly, unhappily.

More sounds he created, projected across the room: "And I suggest that the best thing for you will be to cooperate with the members of the BrathelLanza when they come to visit you."

"The what?" Mathers asked.

"BrathelLanza. You'll find out what it is in due time. For now, cooperate with them as fully as possible, for from cooperating with them will come answers to the questions you want to ask of me, and a means of action."

"A means of action?" Mathers asked stupidly.

"Yes, a means of action, the action that will bring . . ." How much could he tell him? How much had *he* been told when he was Eric Mathers? "Well, you'll see." He could not repress another chuckle he created. There was some degree of humor in the situation. Mathers would see it. When he got here himself. In time.

He had said all he could. He had told Mathers enough. Now Mathers would do the rest of it himself. Mathers would do what had to be done so that the proper sequence of events would take place, so that months in the "future" Mathers would find himself in the recording studio when the police raided the Underground, so that he would be left alone and, with the aid of sense-altering drugs and mnemonic amplification, he would be forced to establish rapport and then resonance with the replicates and . . .

And the Shadowy Man would be born.

The Shadowy Man withdrew from the damp cell that contained Eric Mathers, withdrew into the blackness that is both outside space and time and is the very stuff upon which they are built.

For moments during which the word "time" was a meaningless noise, the Shadowy Man hung suspended, thinking, understanding, knowing. There it was. All laid out before him. There were things he would have to do. Within himself he chuckled, remembered words spoken by the Tromas of KHL-000, words that had seemed like madness to the Eric Mathers who had heard them, words that now the Shadowy Man understood.

The Tromas had said: "What we see is some great power behind this Shadowy Man, some great power that may not yet have even come into existence, that is reaching back through time to alter events—perhaps it is altering events in order to bring itself into existence."

The Tromas had said: "This is a universe of probabilities, Eric. *Probabilities*. Higher orders and lower orders of probability. It is a universe in which the *future* can reach back into the past in order to increase its *probability*. Lower orders of probability can become, through their own manipulation, higher orders of probability. This is so. Kriths know that."

The Tromas had said: "This power is reaching back in time, we believe, in order to manipulate you and those you come in contact with toward some dark future end that is involved with, in some way we do not yet fathom, the *possible* destruction of the entire Krithian race!"

The Tromas had said: "Your Shadowy Man is trying to kill us, Eric."

Yes, the Tromas had known, had understood.

Now *he* did too. He knew what he must do: bring about the past as he knew it, had experienced it as Eric Mathers, to force the past to bring about the present, to force the past to create the Shadowy Man so that he could . . . undo other pasts.

There are no paradoxes in time, he told himself. It is just that no one before me has had any conception of what it is. Though the Tromas do have a glimmering, I have a little more than that.

He set out to do what he knew he would have to do to assure his own creation. . . .

17
Downtime

Through a universe that earlier had seemed to be a blackness but now did not seem so black, for now he could discern in it more and more detail, various shades of blackness and innumerable fragments of light, pinpoints and glows of three-dimensional light as they had made/did make/would make their way through time and space; a void that was the very stuff of which continuua are made. Moving in it, through it, was everything that ever had been, everything that ever would be, everything that ever might have been.

The Shadowy Man moved himself, his awareness, his consciousness backward in time, outward in paratime, searching for a particular point in the multidimensional matrices of time and space and paratime, searching, finding. . . .

A plush villa outside a French town named Beaugency on Timeline RTGB-307, the early morning of 6 April 1972.

During the night the Kriths had sent a contingent of their own Timeliners and local British forces up the River Loire toward the villa presently inhabited by Imperial Count Albert von Heinen and his wife. Under cover of darkness and a surprise British attack, the Timeliners were to capture Von Heinen and his American wife and return them to the Kriths for questioning.

All had gone well enough at first. The Timeliner mercenaries had captured Von Heinen, though only after wounding him, and had gotten his wife without injuring her. But a paratime craft of strange design and capabilities had moved against them, had forced them into a pitched battle that required retreat back to RTGB-307 and the villa.

Now there was gunfire in the distance, the rapid sounds of automatic weapons, the slower noises of semiautomatic ones, the sound of a remote internal-combustion engine dwindling in the distance. Some of the Timeliners had escaped, and in doing so had drawn away the unknown attackers.

As the light of dawn spread across the villa and the stables behind it, figures were moving toward the stables in which there were no horses now, but three staff motorcars of the army of the Holy Roman Empire, brightly polished and immaculately clean, ready for instant use by the officers should they be needed.

One of the figures was a tall blond man in British uniform, who staggered slightly under the weight of the wounded man he carried. There was a determined, half-angry expression on his face, and now and again he glanced at the woman who accompanied him.

Dressed only in a heavy robe, she was a fair-haired woman of medium height, an attractive woman whose green eyes flashed anger and hatred, who glanced at the blond man with bitter lines around her eyes and mouth. She was doing as he told her, but reluctantly.

The man in the British uniform stopped just short of the stables, lowered the wounded man to the ground, ordered the woman to stay with him, and went into the stables to investigate. After a few moments of searching, he found the three motorcars, each decked out with the flag of a *Feldmarschall* of the Imperial Army. He smiled to himself for a moment before going back to where the woman and the wounded man waited.

The Shadowy Man once again took bits of material substance, molecules of air and pieces of floating dust, took them and shaped them with psionic force to create the hazy form that Mathers would later come to know so well. Back in the shadows of the cavernous stables, he bent waves of light, photonic particles, created *himself,* and waited.

When Eric Mathers got back to where Sally Beall von Heinen sat on the ground beside the still figure of the man who was nominally her husband, he holstered his pistol and bent to lift the unconscious man to his shoulder again. Then to Sally he said: "Go on. Get in the first car."

With resignation on her face, the young countess preceded the mercenary along the front of the stables to where the cars were parked.

"Can you drive?" Mathers asked.

"No," Sally von Heinen replied.

"I don't believe you," Mathers said with annoyance. "Get in front. Are the keys in it? Don't lie again."

"Yes, they are."

Mathers dumped the unconscious Von Heinen in the back seat and climbed in beside him. "Okay, let's go," he said.

The motorcar started at once. The Shadowy Man knew that Mathers was pleasantly surprised by this, considering the state of the art of motorcars on this Line. Sally shifted into gear and slowly pulled out of the stables and onto the driveway that led back around the villa's main structures.

"Head toward Beaugency for the moment," commanded the Timeliner mercenary.

He did not speak again for a moment, his eyes going back into the stables, a strange, puzzled expression on his face. For a few moments he peered at the smoky, hazy form in the shadows at the rear of the stables, seeing the image of a human form that the Shadowy Man had built out of air and dust and light. Something that may have been fear went over Mathers' face and his hand reached for the weapon on his hip.

The Shadowy Man loosened his grip on the air, dust, and light. A movement of breeze. The hazy shape was gone.

"What is it?" Countess von Heinen was asking.

"Nothing. Go on."

The car moved on, away from the stables, around the main house, away.

The Shadowy Man smiled within himself, and withdrew. . . .

He moved. Not far through space and time now: a few miles across space, a few hours uptime, no motion at all across paratime. He would not speak yet, would not interfere. There was no need for interference yet. The crucial moments of time and paratime were yet to come. Now he would observe. And let Mathers gradually begin to become aware of him. Later he would speak, when it was necessary. For now . . .

Under Mathers' direction, Sally had driven the German motorcar to a rural wooded area of wartorn France remote from the scene of the battle of the night before. Leaving Sally and the wounded Count tied with ropes, Mathers had then slipped away into the forest, where he had assembled a compact radio transceiver and made contact with the Krithian-Timeliner base of operations in the Outer Hebrides.

"Eric?" asked a Krith's voice from the radio earphone.

"Yes, Kar-hinter, late, but reporting."

"Are you safe?"

"For the moment."

"Count von Heinen?"

"Alive, the last time I looked. I don't know how long he'll last, though." Then he asked about the other Timeliners who had survived the firefight with the strange men from the alien skudder.

"Safe. They managed to get through the Imperial lines just after dawn. Hillary is in a field hospital now. He will be fine, the doctors say."

"Good. Did they tell you what happened?"

"Yes, but they could give no explanations. Can you?"

The Shadowy Man was nothing more than a *pres-*

ence now, a focalization of mental forces at a spot near Mathers. There was nothing visible of him, but Mathers seemed to become aware of him anyway. He looked up, curious, puzzled, worried.

Within himself the Shadowy Man was satisfied. That was sufficient.

"No," Mathers finally said into the transmitter microphone. "It doesn't make any sense. I've never seen a skudder like the one they were in."

"Nor I, from the descriptions." The Krith paused. "Can you tell me where you are?"

"Somewhere in France."

Kar-hinter advised Mathers to take Von Heinen and his wife into hiding if he could find a suitable place and then wait while radio triangulation determined their exact location. Then a skudder would be sent in to retrieve them.

The Shadowy Man withdrew, moved himself uptime, across space. All was going well, exactly as he remembered it. As yet he would not have to interfere. In a few hours, as seen by Eric Mathers, the people who had already made an attempt to rescue Sally and Von Heinen would try again—and this time they would be successful, and would take Mathers their captive. That is how it would happen; that is how it must happen.

Then he, the Shadowy Man, would come to watch, to assist when it was time to assist.

He moved toward a particular point in time, caught it, froze it, moved carefully into it. . . .

He forced matter and energy to form again the hazy figure, this time in the rear of a large hangar on the surface of the earth, above the underground complex called Staunton.

Now Mathers had escaped from Sally and had entered the hangar, where he hoped to gain access to a radio that he could use to once again contact Kar-hinter in the Outer Hebrides, to inform him of the existence of Staunton and the Paratimers.

What the Shadowy Man saw was: Eric Mathers holding a gun on a uniformed technician, forcing him before him across the floor of the hangar toward a craft shaped like a flattened egg, a sautierboat, a machine much like the skudders of the Kriths and Timeliners, yet in some ways very different.

The technician opened the hatch of the large craft and stood for a moment, waiting for Mathers to tell him what to do.

"Get in," Mathers said, gesturing with his weapon.

Then, as the technician obeyed, Mathers' eyes opened wider, for he had caught sight of the hazy figure in the deep shadows at the end of the hangar. Fear went across his features. He spun toward the image, leveling his pistol.

The Shadowy Man released his grip, and the air and light ceased to form the smoky image.

Mathers looked into the shadows, more puzzled than ever, then shook his head and entered the sautierboat behind the technician, to use the radio inside the craft. . . .

Only minutes uptime now, the Shadowy Man moved, the same point in space. . . .

Though now the appearance of the hangar had greatly changed: the Paratimers had discovered what he was doing, and had rushed forces into the hangar to deal with him before it was too late, with hand-weapons of astonishing power.

Now the egg-shaped sautierboat was a mass of ruined, smoldering, twisted metal, and something flammable inside the craft was burning, giving off clouds of smoke that boiled out into the hangar. Men moved about, some carrying fire extinguishers, attempting to put out the fire.

Other men stood above the torn, bloody figure they

had dragged from the wreckage, a mutilated thing that was Eric Mathers, who might be dying.

"Listen to me, bastard," said the man called Scoti who knelt beside him. "If you hurt Sally, I'll see that you live. You'll live so that I can slowly take you apart piece by piece."

Scoti rose, his fists knotted in anger, kicked the inert form savagely, then turned away when a man yelled from near the open front of the hangar: "Scoti, look up there!"

"What is it?" He moved toward the hangar's open doors.

"Airships. British airships."

"Call Mica! Full alert!"

The men dispersed, seeking shelter and more weapons. From the approaching airships, silvery, cigar-shaped, rigid and metallic, gondolas extending almost the full length of their undersides, bombs began to fall, machine guns began to chatter.

The hangar suffered a few near misses and one direct hit that rained fragments of steel and burning wood down over the ruined sautierboat and the still form of Eric Mathers.

The Shadowy Man moved, grasped air between psionic hands, shaped it, moved it, made a voice speak into Mathers' ear, a voice that was very much like Mathers' own voice, and what the voice said was:

"Stay alive, Eric. For God's sake, man, hang on just a little while longer. They're coming to help you. The pain won't last long. You can stand it, Eric. *I did.*"

This crucial point had been reached, achieved. The Shadowy Man had done what he could, now, here. The British airships would land, Mathers' Timeliner confederates would rescue him, find Sally, and take them both from Staunton before the Paratimers who defended the underground city saw that the situation was hopeless and destroyed it. The Shadowy Man withdrew. . . .

Upward in time to the next day, across space to another place, from North America to South Africa, to a hospital room in which Eric Mathers, drugged and bandaged, lay in uneasy sleep, nightmares passing through his mind.

The Shadowy Man touched the mind of the sleeping man, established a brief resonance, spoke to him without words, but tried to tell him that in time he would have the answers, in time he would be able to see through all the shams, the lies, the deceptions, the facades that the Kriths had built, would build, and the facades that the Paratimers had also built. In time he would see, but to do that he would have to survive.

He knew that little of this would get through to Mathers, and that much of what did would be mixed and confused with the nightmares he was experiencing. But some of it would remain, aiding and reinforcing other things that were slowly coming into his mind, awarenesses that would only later blossom into realizations. For a while now Eric Mathers would be on his own, would have to begin finding some of the truths for himself.

Again he withdrew across time and space and paratime . . . to a place months later in chronological time, worlds away in parallel time. . . .

Now a battle raged in a moving skudder. Mathers fought to escape from the Krith named Tar-hortha and the men with him who had captured him and Sally, had separated them, and now carried him across the Timelines toward a destination they had not revealed to him. He fought back.

Feigning drugged unconsciousness, he had slipped into augmentation and had taken a weapon from an unsuspecting guard, had swept the interior of the moving skudder with furious blasts of energy, set off an explosion that had blown away the hand of a giant named Marth, killed a guard named Sulla, and with an energy pistol he had burned to pieces a half-man named Mager.

Now he stumbled over broken flesh and writhing bodies and reached the skudder's hatch, undogged it, jerked it open—and was hit by something like a wind that was blowing out of the inner regions of a frozen hell.

"You did it before," he said aloud to himself, "and it didn't kill you. Dammit, man, you can do it again." But other expressions raced across his face, consternation, disbelief, fear. . . .

The Shadowy Man forced a nucleus of energy into the skudder, held with it as it flickered from world to world. Now he would have to interfere again, would have to act, would have to make certain that when Eric Mathers leaped from this skudder, it was at exactly the right moment, the right place along the Lines. If he failed to do that . . . Well, he couldn't fail.

As Mathers stood uncertainly in the open hatch, looking out at the flickering nothingness of rapidly passing worlds, the injured Krith within the cabin behind him began to move; he reached out a sable-brown hand to grasp Mathers' left ankle. The sounds that came from the Krith's full-lipped mouth were not English, were not Shangalis, were not even coherent. Mathers glanced back at the Krith and saw the mouth open in savage rage, rows of sharp teeth like those of a great cat coming to tear at his flesh.

And his gaze went on beyond the Krith to the shadowy, almost formless figure of the Shadowy Man's focuses of energy.

Now! the Shadowy Man yelled wordlessly to Mathers, exerting a force against him that steeled Mathers' mind and blew like a chill wind against his back.

Mathers jerked his ankle from Tar-hortha's grasp, plunged, leaped, and fell into nothingness right in the middle of a *flicker!*

He was gone. But the Shadowy Man knew exactly where he was, and went to join him. . . .

Hours uptime now, on the world into which Mathers had leaped from the skudder.

It was dark and it was raining. Drugged, battered, beaten, the beginnings of fever in his body, Mathers lay on the sodden ground, no longer caring whether he lived or died.

The Shadowy Man created a voice out of the air and made it speak the same words he had spoken to Mathers before, another time, another place:

"Stay alive, Eric. For God's sake, man, hang on just a little while longer. They're coming to help you. The pain won't last long. You can stand it, Eric. *I did.*"

He remained there for a while, watching the slow breathing, the rain falling, hearing a distant booming across remote hills. They would come. He would live. . . .

Uptime again, some weeks, across space, some miles . . .

This one too would be critical. . . .

A place called Tapferkeitenhaven, a miniature medieval German castle transported to the New World and the Imperial Colony of Sclavania, a few miles south of the New East Anglia border: Von Heinen slept quietly but Mathers could not sleep; there was too much on his mind. He lay back on the soft bed, staring at the white ceiling, and he wondered how many plots were going on in this castlelike home of the Sclavanian Herr Jurgen, how many different webs were being spun and broken, how many. . . .

A point of energy moved through the corridors of Tapferkeitenhaven, observed the stealthy approach of two figures, a man and a woman, both with energy weapons in their hands. They were coming to do some killing.

The nucleus of energy flows moved into the room where the two men lay, not quite forming into the shadowy figure Mathers had seen before, but allowing a tension to build in the air that would bring Mathers out of his reverie, would bring him to full wakefulness so that he might know of the approaching assassins.

Mathers stirred, was aware. He moved, alerted his combat augmentation, slipped from the bed to the floor, knelt and drew a pistol from the drawer of the nightstand between the two beds, then rose to his feet. Outside, the assassins spoke in whispered Shangalis. Now Mathers was certain that Timeliner agents were coming to kill him. He was ready. He went into augmentation. The world slowed, reddened.

The door slowly opened and a heavy man named Otto and a woman named Fredericka stood framed in the yellow torchlight from the hall. Mathers could see Timeliner energy pistols in their hands.

Mathers pulled the trigger. The pistol loudly threw a heavy leaden slug into the face of the heavyset man. As his skull dissolved under the impact of the spreading lead, Mathers cocked the single-action pistol, pulled the trigger again, and put the second slug into the left breast of the pretty little blonde. Fredericka staggered backward, living seconds longer than Otto, long enough to pull the trigger of her own weapon and send a burst of furious coherent energy coruscating across the room, above Mathers' left shoulder.

He was temporarily blinded as he fired the third slug, but was later to find that it had hit the girl just above the navel, exiting through a shattered spine.

As he came out of augmentation, Von Heinen was coming up from the floor, to which he'd rolled during the shooting, crying, "What the hell's going on?"

"Timeliners," Mathers told him quickly. "They tried to kill us." He shoved the smoking pistol into Von Heinen's hand. "Tell them you did it."

"Why?"

"I'll explain later. Take the credit now."

Then Anglianers and liveried servants of Herr Jurgen began rushing into the room.

That's sufficient, thought the Shadowy Man, and disengaged himself from this moment of time, this fragment of space. . . .

The raid was in progress when the Shadowy Man again froze a slice of time and entered it. . . .

Then a firefight was raging in the Krithian skudder pool at Fort Lothairin. Devoto Baugh, Mica, Kjemi Stov and a handful of Paratimers attempted to prevent Mathers' theft of a skudder. Anglianers and Albert von Heinen had died, but Mathers had made his way through blood and flame to take command of a skudder. And as Mica took mortal wounds, bullets from his weapon penetrated the base of Mathers' skudder, damaging it, slowing its escape.

The skudder pool's lights surged to full brilliance, illuminating the broken, bloody tableau. Kjemi Stov—whom Mathers had believed to be a Paratimer, but who was something else—was now in augmentation and charged toward the skudder with a cry of insane rage on his lips, the words he yelled in the Shangalis of the Timeliners.

And into the bright and bloody skudder pool charged the troop that had waited until this moment to spring their trap, a troop of blue-clad Timeliners with energy weapons, olive-clad Sclavanians firing slug throwers, all led by a sable-skinned Krith with a look of fury and of triumph on his flat features, Tar-hortha!

He too was in X5 augmentation and he yelled above the roar, screaming in Shangalis—Mathers thought he could hear him even through the skudder's dome: "You have lost, Eric. You have lost again."

Still moving as only a man in augmentation can, though wounded twice, Mica fired his submachine gun once more before he died, not into the Anglianers so much as through them toward the Krith and his augmented Timeliners. Energy weapons replied to his slug thrower—and Mica's mutilated body seemed to explode in their blaze.

Kjemi Stov, untouched by the lead and energy bursts that swept the shed, had almost reached the skudder. Now Tar-hortha was close behind him.

And as Mathers screamed out his fury at Mica's dying retaliation, the Shadowy Man reached out with a mental probe into the wrecked circuits of the skudder's base, examined the circuits, analyzed them, and drew out of his Mathers-memory schematic diagrams and wiring charts. The circuits were not destroyed, though nearly so. And to repair them, if but briefly and barely, would require a great deal more of him than the mere forming of a shadowy figure or the creation of sound vibrations in the air. The Shadowy Man was not a material being, but he could produce limited effects on matter. So, he applied force here, then there, twisting atoms and molecules, grabbing flowing electrons and moving them. . . .

Mathers knew that something was happening in the circuits, the wiring, the generators of the skudder under him. A scream to match his own, a yell, a roar of mechanical pain, came from them. Lights flickered erratically across the panels. His hands fell to the controls, but he did not know what to do.

Ignoring Kjemi Stov, Tar-hortha had come to a stop only a short distance from the skudder, and looked at Mathers through the glasslike dome, a strange expression on his alien features.

Even as one portion of the Shadowy Man's mind worked to provide some small repair to the damaged skudder, to get it moving at least across a few Lines of Time, another portion of his mind again took air and light and formed them in a smoky, hazy form, a wraithlike shape between the skudder and Tar-hortha.

The Krith showed momentary terror, stepped back, struggled with himself.

From inside the skudder Mathers saw the Shadowy

Man, but also felt the skudder's attempts at moving out of this Line. Then, suddenly, the world outside the skudder grayed. It did not exactly flicker, but the world outside was gone—the Krith, his Timeliners, the bloody skudder pool—and for a few moments there was nothing, nothing at all but grayness.

Mathers was moving across the Lines, but . . .

The Shadowy Man withdrew. The skudder would not go far in paratime, but far enough. And the Krith would move with it, self-skudding until the skudder reached the Line that both Tar-hortha and the Shadowy Man knew it would reach, must reach, or both memory and precognition were wrong. As would the Krith after him, the Shadowy Man went there, across paratime, uptime a matter of minutes to . . .

A large room in a huge building on a world known only to the Kriths, a secret kept even from their Time-liners. Into the room came Eric Mathers, forcing Tar-hortha before him, a pistol at the Krith's back. With them were six machines of grayish metal, the building's guardian robots, watching Mathers in a way that could almost be called suspicious. Inside the room they had entered were some half-dozen large cargo skudders.

"We are here now, Eric," Tar-hortha said, stopping and gesturing toward the skudders. "I suggest that you allow me to set the controls of one of them for you. It will carry you to our destination."

"I'll do my own control setting," Mathers said calmly.

"It would be very unwise for you to do anything other than what I suggest."

"Your robots?" Mathers asked.

"They will see that no harm comes to me."

Three of the devices moved closer to Mathers, raising their metal arms in a manner that could have been menacing.

"Put the foolish pistol away and come with me," Tar-hortha said.

The robots moved closer.

"I'm going to have some answers," Mathers told him.

"Of course you are, but killing me will not give them to you."

"And if I do as you say . . . ?"

"You will be my prisoner, of course."

"I won't put myself in that position again, Tar-hortha."

"I believe you already have."

A metal hand shot out from one of the faceless machines and clamped down suddenly on Mathers' right wrist. He tried to jerk away, to pull himself out of its grasp, but another of the machines came up behind him, grasped both his arms above the elbows, and pulled him backward.

"Tar-hortha!" Mathers screamed in anger. Pain reddened his vision as he fought against the machines that held him, as he willed his right hand to move against the pain, as he swung the barrel of the pistol a few inches to the left, as he pulled back on the trigger. . . .

The roar of the pistol was sudden and loud in the room's near silence, unexpected and terrible.

Mathers felt the bone snap in his wrist and saw his fingers release their hold on the pistol. But, dammit, I've done something! he thought.

Tar-hortha was screaming shrilly, staggering away, clutching at an arm broken between the wrist and elbow, red, manlike blood gushing from the open wound. He slowly dropped to his knees; in his eyes were only fear and horror, for he had been hurt, hurt by a human being, and that was something that never, never happened to a Krith.

"You will die, Eric!" he cried, resting now on his knees, blood pooling below him. "You will die!"

And with the words, the four gray robots moved toward Mathers to aid the two that held him, one by his upper arms, one by his broken wrist.

The pain was coming to him now, and along with it vertigo and nausea. So he'd never know. Now he'd . . .

A grayness came over the room, which for a moment he thought was caused by the pain, by the coming loss of consciousness. He thought he was going under and would probably never awaken again. Yet . . .

The Shadowy Man did not force air and light into the shape of a spectral figure. There was no need for that this time. The vibrations he had set up in the air would have to be sufficient, for there were other things he had to do.

"This isn't the way it should be done, Eric," he forced the air to say, "but there's no other way now."

Mathers attempted to speak; his mouth worked, but no sounds came from it.

The Shadowy Man formed six projections of himself and aimed them toward each of the six machines. The repairs he had performed on the damaged skudder had been difficult enough, but this . . . he had never done anything like this before, dividing himself into so many parts. He was uncertain of how to go about it, uncertain of how long he could remain so fragmented and still coordinate the six separate sets of activities. But there was nothing else he could do.

Each psionic extension found a robot, slipped through its metal skin, sought out its central control system, its computer, its brain, studied it, examined it, tried to find ways of deflecting flows of electrons, of creating pathways within the solid-state modules, of finding a means of temporarily incapacitating the various devices. He found them, the ways of doing what he wished, and the six fragments of his composite personality pushed subatomic particles into places where they had not been before, made electrons flow in pathways not designed for them. But he had not imagined how difficult it would be.

"Quickly now," he forced the air to say. "I can hold them only for moments!"

Mathers extricated himself from the machines as they stopped, then reversed their motion. He dragged himself to his feet, looked at his limp right hand dangling from the broken wrist, then looked at the Krith who knelt in a pool of his own blood.

"The gun, Eric!" the Shadowy Man said with vibrations of air.

Mathers nodded, seemed to regain some control of himself, and bent to grasp the gun in his left hand.

"Hurry!" the air said. "We haven't long."

Mathers stood up, holding the pistol awkwardly. "Into that skudder," he told the Krith, shaking his head to clear it as he moved toward Tar-hortha.

The Kirth shook his head in a very human fashion.

Mathers pointed the revolver at the Krith's face, only inches away. Tar-hortha sighed deeply through wide, wet lips, then he slowly came to his feet.

For a few moments more the Shadowy Man held the six machines immobile, long enough for Mathers to force the wounded Krith into the skudder and then climb in himself. That was long enough. Mathers could make it now. He let the robots go.

With a mental sigh, he relaxed for a moment, watched as the robots approached the skudder, as the skudder hummed and then, with a clap like thunder, slipped out of that universe and into another and then another, skudding across the Lines of Time.

The Shadowy Man relaxed, but not for long. There was one more encounter, one more place in time and space where his destiny was fixed, where he must go, for the memory of Eric Mathers told him that he must go there, must do things there, must fight and perhaps . . . Well, there was no knowing the outcome. He would learn.

Summoning his strength, he pulled himself out into the speckled blackness of Notever, Nowhen, and prepared to move uptime again, across the Lines to KHL-000 and the confrontation with the Tromas, who ruled the race of Kriths.

18

The First Confrontation

KHL-000. The Krithian Homeline. The most prime of all the Prime Lines. The fountainhead from which issued the decisions and the commands that altered uncounted worlds across the Lines, that affected billions upon billions of human beings across those worlds. The seat and source of the power of the Kriths. And the residence world of the Tromas, the twelve females of the race who were its guiding force.

It was toward KHL-000 that the Shadowy Man moved, toward a place in time where Eric Mathers was now a captive of the Kriths. In exchange for answers to his questions and his reunion with Sally, the Tromas expected him to lure the Shadowy Man to KHL-000. In truth, the Shadowy Man knew, they wished him to come to KHL-000 so that they might hold him and destroy him, forever ridding themselves of the danger to their plans that he represented.

Yet he went there. There may have been fear in him, but if there was he submerged it, pushed it away from himself. There was no time for fear now. He knew that he *must* go to KHL-000: his going there was in Mathers' memory, his going there had enabled Mathers and Sally to escape the Kriths, had allowed Mathers to complete the circuit that had brought the Shadowy Man into existence. He had no choice but to go there and risk exposing himself to the Kriths. And if there existed in Mathers' memory something that indicated the defeat and destruction of the Shadowy Man, there was not absolute certitude in it; Mathers had not *known* that the Shadowy Man was destroyed, but

158

merely that his presence, after a terrible battle with the Tromas, was no longer there upon KHL-000. What might have become of him then, Mathers had not known, had had no way of knowing. So there was the hope in him, as he pushed his intelligence across time and space and paratime once more, that his defeat might not be total. Perhaps Mathers had known nothing of the *final* outcome of the battle between the Shadowy Man and the Tromas. He felt deep within the essence of himself that there was a great deal more to come that neither Mathers nor himself had yet suspected. He would see. . . .

Now: A room in a towering building, a spire that climbed toward the sky; a bedroom that was part of the suite that the Kriths had given Sally Beall von Heinen after bringing her across the Timelines and using her as bait to bring Eric Mathers to them.

Within the room was a bed on which lay Mathers and Sally, now sensing the approach of *something*.

In a far corner of the bedroom, a manlike shape formed, a thing only half visible in the gloom, hazy, ghostly, half immaterial, but it was a *presence* and the two people in the room were aware of it.

He collected himself, forced concentrations of himself into the modified air, the bending light. It had been harder to enter KHL-000 than he had anticipated; it had been farther across the Lines than he had realized, and there were forces here, powers and protections, that he had not realized could exist. But he had overcome them and he was there. He made the air speak:

"It was very difficult this time, getting here. I didn't think it would be that hard."

"Eric!" Sally cried, as she dropped the sheet she had pulled around herself and drew herself toward Mathers.

"It's okay," the man said. "I know who it is."

"That—that's your voice, Eric," Sally stammered, whispering.

The Shadowy Man again made the air speak for him: "There is little time. And the forces involved in this are beyond your present comprehension. In moments, if not already, the Tromas will know I'm here, and then . . . Well, you've got to get out of here, the two of you."

"Out of here?" Mathers asked stupidly.

In exasperation the Shadowy Man said: "That's why I came—to rescue the two of you! There's a way to escape, and if you'll listen to me I'll tell you how to do it."

"We're listening," Mathers replied from the bed.

"Very well," the Shadowy Man said; and, selecting fragments from the Mathers-memory he held, he told them how to get from Sally's apartment to the roof of the towering spire, of a half-secret stairway that would take them up to where there would be "a means of escape" awaiting them—best not yet to further confuse them with the nature of their escape route, which the Shadowy Man himself did not yet fully understand. He told them that there would be guards and obstacles before them but that he would do everything he could to pave the way for them.

"And then what?" Mathers asked, an awkward, strained sound to his voice.

"You escape. What you do after that is up to you, Eric, and you, Sally. I can't tell you what to do once you escape this Line. I've already done far more than I should have. I'm not yet certain just where in the orders of probability—or improbability—" He found that he could not help but chuckle at the confusion he felt in himself and was passing on to Mathers and Sally. "—all this lies anyway—we may one day find out that none of it has happened anyway."

"What do you mean?" Mathers asked in confusion.

"Nothing," answered the Shadowy Man, now becoming certain that the Tromas were aware of his presence in KHL-000, and that they would certainly be doing something about it soon, terribly soon.

Even as he prepared to speak again he could feel something moving in the world outside the apartment, a force swelling, expanding, probing toward him, carefully at first, hesitant, then more certain of itself.

"Now you must work out some simple ruse to distract the guards outside the doors of the apartment," he told them quickly. "Sally, you can help in this. Draw them into the room. Get their attention. Then perhaps Eric can do something. And remember, they have no women of their own." He thought briefly of the Magers, as Mathers had called them, not Kriths in disguise as he had once believed, but something else, almost men, but not quite men, something more, or perhaps something less, maybe a hybrid of man and Krith, certainly not the product of any known evolutionary process. But then neither were the Kriths. "And remember, they have no women of their own," he had said; "they're drawn to human women, some of them."

Sally made a motion as if to speak, but then did not, suddenly aware of a second *presence,* a new and terrible force gathering around the Shadowy Man.

He felt it too, a touch, lightly at first, no more than a brushing, then a first contact, a quick and ruthless examination. A pause. A flickering of fire across an endless sky. A swelling of anger and hatred. A rushing toward him. A further swelling. Then the lash of a whip of great psionic force across his consciousness.

He almost lost control of the air for a moment, then made it speak for him: "They know!"

The lash came again, and with it the swelling of pain, psychic pain of an intensity such as he had never before known or imagined. Then a momentary pause. He looked within himself to see what defenses he had, what weapons with which to strike back.

And with it all was a momentary sense of resonance

with the Eric Mathers who was still on the bed with Sally. A brief sharing of pain and awareness.

Mathers gasped aloud in that common pain.

"Eric!" Sally cried.

A momentary respite, the raising of a mental shield. The Tromas withdrew for instants, preparing to strike again, and harder.

"You're me," Mathers said.

The Shadowy Man made the air speak again: "In a sense. You might be me. You might become me, given time."

Mathers was there with him for instants more: Mathers looking forward in time, backward through the Shadowy Man's own memories. Fear!

Then he pushed Mathers away, out of him, knowing that Mathers could never withstand what he could feel sweeping toward him across space from the palace of the Tromas.

Lightning flashed in the bedroom, leaping from some point near the ceiling toward the focus of his consciousness. And with it the blow of a psionic ax, the cutting, ripping, tearing through him of a sharpened blade of mental force. He erected his shields, strengthened them, struggled to hold himself together until the swift and terrible pressure subsided.

Blazing with a halo of light and invisible radiation, the Shadowy Man made the air say: "I will fight them as long as I can, but I don't know how long that will be. I'm a long way from home. . . ." Another blow was coming. Lightning crackled through the room. "Hurry!" the air cried.

Mathers pulled himself from the bed, drew Sally after him, and, both of them naked, they stumbled from the bedroom as forces swept through it, blasting, shattering, rending.

"Come on," Mathers called, his voice dwindling as the blow came toward the Shadowy Man, sweeping toward him, then across him, battering again at his shield, being partly held this time, only portions of the psionic attack bursting through to shatter, to shake him, to rip through him and fill him with pain.

He forced the shields up once more, swung them forward to deflect streams of psionic flame, sought again for weapons, found them, curled balls of coruscating energy within himself, outside the universe, and sucked them into space/time to hurl them at the Tromas.

With the shields before him he advanced, feet, miles, light-years; the terms are meaningless. He advanced toward the Tromas.

The Krithian females drew together their own strength, united again, raised their own shields, and moved forward to meet him.

Through space and time he hurled the particles/waves/balls/stars/novas/quasars of psionic force toward the advancing Tromas . . . who caught them and hurled them back at him, splashing across his shields, sending him reeling backward, ripping again through his consciousness.

The Shadowy Man, stunned by the sudden reversal, retreated. The nucleus of his energy floated, drifted, moved relative to spatial frameworks.

Into the living room of the suite came the form of the Shadowy Man, his smoky, ghostly form now clothed in flickering lightning and halos of incandescence; sheets of auroral flame surrounded him, flickering in neon colors across the spectrum from the edges of infrared to the margins of ultraviolet. The air around him was becoming ionized; carpeting and woodwork smoldered as he brushed across them, moving ever more slowly and ponderously, struggling to halt his retreat, to turn back toward his enemies, to again try to find weapons to use against them.

Other weapons he did find, and hurled the strength of them outward, but with ease the Tromas seemed to catch them and throw them back against his shields.

They were powerful, unimaginably powerful, these females of the Krithian race. How had he ever thought he could equal them in combat?

But he could not yield, not yet. For a while he must hold. He must give Mathers and Sally time to escape, for if they did not escape, there would never be a Shadowy Man. The universe looped and looped within itself. What was it Mathers had once said? "The universe is a can of worms, and each worm is bending back upon itself to eat its own tail. . . ."

For a moment there was respite again. For an instant the Tromas did not hurl wave after wave of psionic energy against him. He gasped within himself, drew himself together, welded back together the shattered margins of his consciousness, tried to find additional means of strengthening his shields, for now he knew that all he could hope to do was hold, for just a bit longer, hold and give Mathers and Sally time. He could not defeat the Tromas. He could barely even strike back at them.

And then there it was, sweeping across space and time again, a tsunami of psionic force, greater than all the others before, a cresting wave of hatred, anger, and destruction; burning, shattering mental forces rushing toward him. The Tromas had gathered all their power in one great field and threw it with all their strength at the conflux of forces that was the Shadowy Man.

He braced himself for the swelling tide of flame.

It came, splashed against his shields, tore against them and then through them, one after the other, ripping them away and plunging deeper and ever deeper toward the remote core of his consciousness.

How do I relate it? How do I tell what it was like to be . . . smashed and battered by psionic blows of tremendous, godlike, unimaginable power, to be struck and struck again and to be almost overwhelmed by the waves of hate and anger from the female Kriths, to feel your composite mind torn to shreds by psionic forces infinitely greater than your own, ancient and more wise in their use of power, to be beaten to your figurative knees and then, screaming in psionic pain, withdraw, fall upward through time, inward across the Lines, back into the subterranean laboratories where your own physical body and those of your replicates are contorted with pain.

How do I tell it? I don't know.

But with that last assault the Shadowy Man could endure no more; he knew that his consciousness was being destroyed and in instants more he would no longer exist and his physical bodies would be nothing more than vegetables with burned-out brains.

With an effort that took more strength than he knew he had, the Shadowy Man disengaged himself, not knowing at the time how he was able to accomplish even that. Mortally wounded, he felt himself, dying, himself and the physical bodies upon whose brains he was built. He fell upward, inward, screaming in the pain he could no longer tolerate, seeking the safety of the underground shelter so that he might die in some semblance of peace.

19

Downtime Again

But he did not die.

The wounds were not mortal. Painful and soul-shattering, yes, but not mortal. The blasts had hurt him, the Shadowy Man, but they had not moved far enough across time and space and paratime to touch the brains of which he was the composite mind.

He fell back to those cerebral cortexes, resonated among them, rested, wept, shuddered in remembered pain, and then, at last, for the first time in his existence, he slept.

When the consciousness of the Shadowy Man again had self-awareness, he knew that he would recover from the ordeal through which he had gone. He would recover and he would do more than that. There was a great deal that he could learn from the experience, a great deal that he could put into practice the next time he encountered the Tromas, for he was certain that he would again encounter them in combat, though exactly where, exactly when, he was yet to know.

He rested, studied, analyzed, gained knowledge and regained strength, and then, for a brief moment, cut himself away from the bodies of the replicates, now relaxing with the passing of the pain they too had felt, and entered complete third-level resonance with the superior of the replicates, the physical Eric Mathers of Here and Now.

The body was still drugged, was still without the ability to move itself, other than to rotate its eyes within their sockets and raise and lower its eyelids.

The Shadowy Man had anticipated this, and was not disturbed.

Through those eyes he again looked out into the recording room within the Underground of the Brathel-Lanza, saw once more the bloodstained body of the dead technician on the floor near the chair, and Mathers' immobile figure, what he could see of it. With the eyes of that body he swept leftward and found once more the chronometer. The digits read 12:42:01. Just over thirty minutes of chronological time had elapsed since he had last looked at the chronometer, before he had begun his series of flights across space and time.

There was, he realized, a definite correlation between time as he experienced it and time as the still body of Eric Mathers experienced it, a correlation, but one of extremely high ratio. There was a linearity to time, he was certain, although time was not linear in the sense that he had once believed it to be. Nor, he suspected, would it be possible for him, the Shadowy Man, to occupy a point in space/time already occupied by himself. Why, he was uncertain, but he believed it to be so. He would have to hold these things in mind and work them into the concepts of the nature of time as he was gradually developing them.

Thirty minutes. Then MaLarba had been dead nearly seventy-two minutes. An hour and twelve minutes had passed since the raid on the Underground had taken place. That still gave him ample time before the drugs began to wear off the body of Eric Mathers.

The drugs had begun to become a matter of concern to him. He was certain that, at least in part, his creation was based on the condition of this physical body, which had been his starting point. The drugs had altered the mind of Eric Mathers, had made that mind more capable of digging into itself, of bringing forth unconscious memories, had made it more sensitive and more receptive to union with the replicates. And the mnemonic recorder, he felt, was also a factor: the electrodes were still attached to Eric Mathers, his so-called brain waves were still being detected by them, passed on to the amplifiers of the recorder, and in the fact of their amplification lay something of the secret of the creation of the Shadowy Man. Many factors had gone into his genesis.

Now he was uncertain of how the wearing off of the mnemonic drugs might affect the resonance patterns between the senior and the replicates. There would be some effect, of that he was certain. But how great? Was it possible that with the passing of the drugs, it would be impossible to maintain the total resonance between the 337 bodies? Might it be that he would disintegrate into merely a senior and a cluster of replicates, a single conscious mind, that of Eric Mathers, and the nearly unconscious minds of the replicates? Would, he was asking, the Shadowy Man cease to exist once the drugs no longer held their sway?

He was not certain. Despite the data that had swelled up out of the unconsciousness of Eric Mathers, there still was not enough information to answer that question. Perhaps there was not enough data anywhere. Who had ever researched this sort of thing? Such a condition had never before existed in all the universes, he believed, outside of the existence of the Tromas themselves, and he was uncertain how close an analogy he could draw between them and himself. Again, too little data.

But that time was centuries away as time was experienced by the Shadowy Man, and there was a universe of things he could do before that much time had gone by.

He set out to do them.

Once again he divorced himself from the physical bodies upon which he was built, existed as a resonance pattern between the senior and the replicates, and once more moved into a psionic void where none of the conventional human senses had any validity, although he had awareness, more awareness than any mere human being could ever have had.

Again he moved outside the framework of ordinary dimensions, outside length, breadth, height, outside chronological time, outside parallel time. Now these terms were all but meaningless, save that he could move about and select whatever dimensional coordinates he might wish, pick out a spot in the continuua, touch it, freeze it, place himself there.

But he did not yet choose to do that. For a while, which could not be measured in terms of the passage of time, he remained without motion, without time, and once more assessed what knowledge he had gained since he had come into existence.

Most of what went through his composite mind could not be expressed in words, perhaps could not be expressed by the symbols of any human mathematics, but one line of thought, the conclusion of his mentation, might have been something like this, had he been using words:

It is obvious that I cannot defeat the Tromas on their own ground, on their own terms. Another encounter such as the last, even with what I have learned, could destroy me. So, I must find a way to meet them on more nearly equal terms. I must find conditions more favorable to me, find the Tromas less ready to fight back against me, find them ignorant of the threat I am to them and ignorant of the powers I possess, perhaps ignorant even of the powers they themselves possess. But where? When?

There were other hazards, he knew. The farther he moved from his time/place of origin, the more tenuous would become the link between himself and his corporeal bodies and weaker would become the powers he could summon. He could not move too far away, but . . .

The Shadowy Man moved outward in space, across paratime, backward in chronological time, downtime to . . . KHL-000 in the chronological past . . . pausing along the way to freeze a fragment of the continuua, to reach into four-dimensional space/time and touch the electronic workings of a vast library computer on a world dominated by the Kriths and their Timeliners. It took him moments or aeons to learn the computer's language, and more moments or aeons to seek out the data he wanted, to separate the truth from the lies. Then, satisfied that he knew what he wished to know—for the moment, at least—the Shadowy Man once more moved downtime. . . .

Years downtime now, centuries into the past as Eric Mathers would have understood the structure of time, back to the year A.D. 1610.

Eric Mathers had visited KHL-000 and had spoken with the ruling females of the Krithian race in the month of February, A.D. 1972, as the calendar was kept on some worlds.

Yet, in some spacio-temporal frameworks, from certain viewpoints, the Kriths themselves did not come into being until the year A.D. 2214, the product of genetic engineering on a Timeline the coordinates of which the Shadowy Man had not yet discovered. The Kriths had been "grown" from human genetic material, engineered to survive on a world very different from any of the Earths across the Lines, a planet of another star, light-years remote in space.

And it had been nearly two centuries later, A.D. 2404, before the descendants of the colonists of UR-427-51-IV fully assessed the power that resided within themselves, commandeered a spaceship and returned to Earth, then self-skudded across the Lines until they found a world to their liking, an Earth they could take over as their own, which they called KHL-000, their first headquarters in paratime.

Close to a century had gone by before the Kriths had decided to go downtime. After finding KHL-000, the few thousand members of the race had lived there for nearly a century before they became aware of the enormity of what would happen when the parachronal potential of the universe would be forced to reorder itself toward simplicity, or cease to exist. Around A.D. 2500 the Kriths somehow brought a chronal-displacement device to KHL-000. And from the KHL-000 of circa A.D. 2500, the entire Krithian race had migrated downtime to circa A.D. 1600, still on KHL-000. And from this vantage point in the "past" they had begun gradually increasing their strength, recruiting humans and then forming the Timeliners to do their work for them. Three and a half centuries later, a vast number of worlds lay under their sway, and more were poised to fall into their orbit.

The Shadowy Man knew his destination: in paratime, KHL-000, once more, in chronotime about the year A.D. 1610. The Kriths would be there, nearly every member of their race, just now beginning to move across the Lines of Time. This would be the place/time to strike, before they had begun their remodeling of tomorrow, perhaps before the Tromas had matured sufficiently to be fully cognizant of their powers.

As he moved through the darkness that he no longer considered black, as he swept across the multidimensional fabric of the universes and neared a destination that could only have been expressed in five or more separate sets of coordinates, certain things for which he was not looking impinged on the Shadowy Man's awareness, things he sought now to ignore—for he did not wish to be distracted from his goal—but which he found he could not totally disregard:

There was a distortion of the universal matrix through which he passed, a confusion, a series of anomalies; in terms of human senses, if such analogies are justifiable: shrieking sounds came out of the stillness, rising along an alien musical scale to vanish and then reappear; splashes of light and color coming and then going, yellows and oranges, explosions of bloody crimson; a flow here of space/time that seemed to turn about upon itself, moaning as it did so, leaking yellows and greens into the blackness, a loop in the stuff of the universe, or perhaps becoming a spiral, a purple, sighing whirlpool. And there was another, spinning off from the first, flashing silver and gold, touched with red, screaming and moaning, creating new and different, unknown and unexpected currents through the non-matter/nonenergy of the continuua. And farther on downtime, still another: vortexes of color and light, of infrared and ultraviolet, of sound and motion, vortexes of confusion wherein time and space and paratime followed not the multibranched, quasilinear progression, but doubled back, meeting themselves again, producing still more eddies in space/time. Then there was a wavefront sweeping forward in time, black and silvery, roaring as does an avalanche, spreading out from a single point in the five-dimensional context, producing still more confusion.

For a few moments, caught up in the bending, looping, swirling stuff upon which the universes are built, he lost his bearings, was unable to pinpoint himself within the five-sided references, felt a weakening not so much of himself as of the medium through which he swam, found it difficult to propel himself through the miasma, as if here, in this Nonplace, Nowhen, there was something that might be described as a tear, a flaw in the matrix.

A kind of fear swept through him. For a moment he was near panic. Was it possible that he might get caught in one of these eddies and be unable to escape, captured forever in a loop in time that had no beginning and no end, that forever doubled back on itself meaninglessly?

Then he regained control of himself, steadied, studied as well as he could the forces at work, and the lack of working forces in other places. For an infinite moment he paused, then charted himself a path. Drifted for a moment. Then propelled himself again across the Nothingness, the Everything.

He was free, and again paused, wondered, speculated. What had happened, what could possibly have taken place here to so disturb the basis of all time and space and paratime? And did he have time to try to determine the answers?

Although "time" was very largely a meaningless term in this context, there was a subjective passage of time to the Shadowy Man, an urgency within him. There were things he had to do, and the sooner he got them done, the better. He realized that despite the powers he had gained in evolving from Eric Mathers into the Shadowy Man, he was still very much a human being in his psychology, still very much hampered by a psychological point of view that saw time as a steady progression from past to present to future, and his consciousness still continued to function as if that progression were true. Perhaps that was the only way a human or human-evolved mind could function. But then, perhaps, once his quest was completed, once his mind was at ease, he could more fully explore this, could come to *feel* as well as *know* that such terms as "past," "present," and "future" really have very little meaning at all.

Later, he told himself, later—and realized that it would be a difficult thing indeed, even for him, to ever fully comprehend a nonlinear view of time.

Again he oriented himself, established once more his five-dimensional position, moved toward his goal, KHL-000, A.D. 1610.

Through the Nowhere, Nowhen, he moved again, passing out of the worst of the confusion and entering into relative blackness, relative silence, across time, space, and paratime, and arriving. . . .

Now, with a mental sigh of relief, the Shadowy Man once more was able to freeze a point in space/time, to focus himself on a single place/event, to involve himself with three-dimensional space, the passage of chronological time.

The spatial viewpoint that the Shadowy Man initially established for himself was akin to that of a low-orbiting satellite above Earth as it existed on Line KHL-000. Below him, the planet turned slowly, a cloud-whitened world, a world of oceans and land, rivers and mountains, forests and deserts.

For a long while he drank in with pleasure the sight of this Earth below him, reveling in the beauty of it. From this height it appeared to be a virgin world, an untouched, unspoiled near-paradise. He was still very much a human being, he thought, as he considered his love for this planet.

Then he began to move his viewpoint, the focus of his consciousness, his vision. Like a spaceship returning from a trip to the stars, he lowered himself toward the planet, entered the atmosphere, and approached the landmasses below.

Even as he came in and then momentarily held himself still, poised but a few miles up, he could see no signs of human habitation—or, in this case, Krithian habitation. Yes, he told himself, they have been here but a few years now, they will have only a few centers of their culture, for theirs is still a very small race, a few thousand individuals now. Their works would hardly be visible from any great distance.

And on Sally's world of A.D. 1610, what works of man would have been visible from this altitude? The Great Wall of China, perhaps. A few of the largest cities, their dim nighttime lights, their daytime smoke, London, Paris, Berlin, Moscow, Peking perhaps, few more, little else.

As he swept closer, now moving like a great-winged bird of prey above the virgin landscape, he wondered where the Kriths would have established their initial settlements. He delved into his memories, the memories of Eric Mathers, and sought.

Remembered . . . that when Mathers had arrived on KHL-000 of A.D. 1972 he had been in North America and it was there that he had been taken captive by the Kriths and their companions, the Mager-types, as he had called them. But a period of unconsciousness had followed his capture and during it he could have been taken just about anywhere on the planet. But had he been?

He dug further into the Mathers-memories. There was no reason to believe that he had been taken from North America, so for the moment he would assume that he had not been. Then what had been the weather, the climate, when Mathers awoke? Warm, pleasant, a day in spring or summer it had seemed, although it should have been late winter, the month of February. Therefore, if he had still been in North America, it must have been in the southern part, perhaps in one of the areas known as Florida or Mexico or California on some worlds.

Poised above the great landmass of Asia, the Shadowy Man turned his consciousness eastward, swept across the Pacific Ocean, approached North America, angled toward the southern coastline. As the water gave way to land, he slowed, stopped, poised, hovered again. Then he slipped a portion of himself out of the electromagnetic spectrum, entered into the semidarkness of psionic awareness, and probed for consciousness: dozens of minds, not the kinds of minds with which he was more familiar, but minds nonetheless—Krithian minds.

And were they aware of him as well, some of them?

He probed again, and found one particular cluster of minds shining more brightly than the others, eleven of them, glowing with psionic awareness, dimly conscious of his presence, he was now convinced, yet not knowing what he was.

With electromagnetic vision again he looked, and correlated this viewpoint with his psionic one. Then he knew where they were.

South he moved along the coastline. Saw them.

Not far from the sandy, rocky shore was a clearing in the trees and brush, not a city by any standards he cared to recall, hardly more than a village, a series of primitive, temporary structures in jumbled, unplanned arrangement. Only two of the structures appeared to have been built with any permanence in mind, and these were hardly more than crudely baked brick, with rough-hewn wooden beams and windows glazed with glass of poor quality. Hardly the majestic cities of KHL-000 that Eric Mathers had envisioned.

But then, he reminded himself again, they were but newly come to this world and as yet had not recruited their vast armies of human assistants. Kriths were a people never given to the building of technological things—a very unmechanical people, the Kriths—and he knew that the cities and the great landscaped parks of KHL-000 that Eric Mathers had seen would not come into being until large numbers of humans worked for the Kriths, until their companions—the semihuman, semi-Krithian Magers—were among them. Now the Kriths dwelt on a technologically primitive level. But, he told himself, it would be very unwise to underestimate them just because they did not have the artifacts of high technology. They had their minds, their ability to self-skud from Line to Line, and they had the Tromas—not yet so ancient and wise in their powers, but the powers were there, and could be used.

He quickly probed toward the two more-permanent-appearing structures.

What he found in the first of them was surprising, though it should not have been. He should have anticipated something like this. It would have been their first order of business.

Inside the structure, which had a primitive look from

the outside, he found ample evidence of the technology
he had seen before. The low, rambling, brick and
wooden structure reminded him very much of some
portions of the Underground of the BrathelLanza.
Rooms here and there were filled with white-smocked
figures—humans! Microscopes and centrifuges, incuba-
tion units and culture containers, equipment for the
analysis and study of unicellular life, row after row of
liquid-filled containers that brought to his mind the
term "encanters," for in these vessels embryos almost
human in their appearance developed outside the
wombs of their mothers. Within this building, as unpre-
possessing as it was, human scientists and technicians,
supervised by adult male Kriths, were growing clones,
Krithian replicates.

Of course, he said to himself, the very first thing
they would do is see to it that their numbers increase:
a race that numbers but a few thousand is hardly ready
to begin remodeling hundreds and hundreds of parallel
Earths. And he remembered the words that the Tromas
had spoken to Eric Mathers once he had realized how
terribly few there were of the female Kriths: "We all
are pregnant. We each give birth at least once a year.
Yet still we are few, terribly few to maintain a race
as widely spread as ours. . . . There are other means of
maintaining our race, of propagating our species. . . .
Once our chances of survival were minimal. You
might find it a wonder that there are Kriths in this
universe at all."

For the first time, the Shadowy Man realized that
the majority of the members of the Krithian race must
be replicates. Perhaps a dozen new individuals would
be born each year, but millions would be needed for
the ever-increasing number of worlds they dominated.
Cloning would be the only answer.

But in a race numerically dominated by clones, he
thought, had there ever occurred a situation analogous
to his own? But then, he thought not. The conditions

that conspired to create the Shadowy Man were, perhaps, unique in all the universes.

He withdrew from the first structure, turned his attention to the second, probed, entered.

Eleven female Kriths, gross, fat, ugly, sat in wheeled chairs in a circle facing inward, carrying on a silent conversation among themselves, when the Shadowy Man entered the room they occupied.

For an instant he was aware of bits of their silent conversation: *For the fifth Line to the Temporal-East of the first Indus Line, I would suggest . . . Would be a very wise move, for our initial objectives there are . . . What we shall call a "Prime Line," the first of many that we must . . .*

Then the conversation ceased in midstream. Before, they had been dimly, vaguely aware of a presence outside themselves, but had not concerned themselves greatly with it. Now they knew *he* was there. Their attention, now focused into what might be considered a single consciousness, turned to him.

Who are you? the Tromas asked.

You don't know? the Shadowy Man asked them.

We do not know. Answer us, who are you?

Have you not looked into your own future? Have you not scanned far uptime?

We have, and . . .

A pause in the voiceless reply. Then what could be described as a soundless cry, an astonishment, a gasp. A babble of separate mental voices: *. . . It cannot be . . . It is* him *. . . But the orders of probability are so low . . . Those probabilities can be altered, we know this . . . Then is it? . . . It is!*

The Shadowy Man realized his mistake. He had waited too long; he had given them an opportunity to recognize him for what he was, could be, would be.

Together, sisters! . . .

Now he was forming a psionic bolt, a mass of furious energy to use against them; he drew it back, launched it toward the clustered female Kriths.

The atmosphere within the building was charged with tension. Balls of lightning skittered across the floor. The smell of ozone grew thick in the air.

The psionic blast slapped against the Tromas, but already their shields were coming up, deflecting most of the energy, converting it to other forms, radiating heat, light, X-rays, and microwave radio energy back into the air, into the sky, into space.

The Shadowy Man dodged backward, prepared another bolt of psionic energy, brought up his own shields . . . only to feel the lash of the Tromas striking out against him, splashing against his shields, sending him reeling.

His shields came up again and once more he rushed toward them, launching his bolts and finding them met by bolts of even greater strength hurled at him by the Tromas.

A second time he retreated, pulled farther away, and felt the Tromas seeking him, probing outward, upward, across time and space. As yet he had suffered no pain, for no significant energies had gotten past his shields, but he could weigh his power against theirs, and he saw that, despite the comparative youth of the Tromas as a psionic entity Here and Now, it was still far older and more experienced than he. Even Here and Now, the Tromas had the capability to defeat him.

It was not cowardice but wisdom that led the Shadowy Man to make his decision to withdraw not only from the direct confrontation with the Tromas but from that space/time itself.

Another place, another set of circumstances more to his liking, would have to be found. He was still meeting the Tromas on their own ground, their own terms, and there was no way he could hope to best them there.

He fled outward, upward, across time and space, toward . . .

He was not yet certain. He would think, consider, decide, and then . . .

Before him, as he moved in the direction he called "uptime," he was again aware of the flux of space/time that he had encountered before, the vortexes and loops, the spirals and pinwheels, the shades of blackness that became great splashes of mingled colors, the sounds of a maddened symphony orchestra, the wavefront of confusion, now followed by still another such wavefront that engendered still more confusion, more loops and swirls in the universal substance.

He paused in his flight, considered, then probed. He reached out, grasped one particular piece of space/time, froze it, peered into it, then sought another and did the same, trying as he did to build within his composite mind some picture of what was taking place within this area of madness in the universal matrix.

What he found was a multitude of conflicting and confusing worlds lying side by side in paratime.

One world, a KHL-000 a century or more uptime from his conflict with the younger Tromas, a place in time that could perhaps have carried the label A.D. 1740 had anyone been able to place the world within the framework of a calendar: a world without intelligent life at all; a world on which men had once lived, long before, but from which they had been removed by forces not totally comprehensible even to the Shadowy Man; a world where forests engulfed ruined castles and hamlets, while the bones of men were dust within ancient tombs.

And beside this world in paratime, a world that would have had the same calendrical label: it was the focus of a conflict, yet not a conflict between men but between Kriths. The Shadowy Man found himself rocked by the improbability of it: Kriths do not fight among themselves. Yet there it was—a Krith who had a large red disk painted on his chest and whose genitals were painted the same color stood silently, with his back to a tree, his eyes scanning the forest before him. Silently another Krith appeared, one with blue-painted genitals and a blue star on his chest, skudding in from another Line (or from another place on this Line? the Shadowy Man wondered), then making a sudden, deadly leap, planting a sharpened stick in the throat of the red-painted one. The victorious Krith gave out a great war whoop; but, as suddenly as he had appeared, two more self-skudded into this place, their genitals and chests painted red. They saw the slain Krith, one of their own kind, and his slayer, decorated with blue, and they pounced on him, driving him to the ground with wooden staffs, battering him until his arms were broken and his skull cracked and a reddish gray muck spilled onto the ground beneath the trees.

Still other worlds, as insane and improbable, in wild juxtaposition, seeming to have no relation to one another as did normal worlds in paratime. He saw worlds where men fought rearguard actions against numerically inferior but technologically superior Kriths; armies of men with muskets and crossbows being wiped out by a single Krith with an energy rifle! Worlds where Krithian overlords, with no apparent desire to dominate other worlds, worked human slaves in vast plantations that grew esoteric crops such as no Earth had ever seen before. Worlds where semibarbaric humans worshiped the sole survivor of the Krithian race, an ancient, nearly senile, alien god-king who knew that when he died, with him would die all the dreams of his vanished race.

An uncountable multitude of worlds branching, splitting, proliferating.

And other worlds of encapsulated time: a world whose history began about A.D. 1610 and would end about A.D. 2500, looping back upon itself and beginning again, meaninglessly; a world so isolated from the rest of the universe that its Krithian inhabitants could not even skud away from it to places of sanity, but were doomed to repeat that slice of 890 years forever.

Another encapsulation: frozen time, no movement at all. There is no life on this Earth. Barren stone, frozen water, unimaginable gulfs of loneliness. Not death. Just nonlife.

The Shadowy Man shuddered in terror, and asked himself how it was possible for such worlds to be. Then realized. As the Kriths should have realized. At least part of it.

The Kriths had come across the parallel worlds and settled on KHL-000 and for a time had lived there, then had decided to go downtime to begin their remaking of the histories of the parallel worlds as early as possible. From their decision to pluck themselves out of space/time and hurl themselves, as a race, backward into the historical past had come this fragmentation. Moving backward in time, passing themselves, as it were, moving through already established historical eras of solely human habitation, they had brought into being a fragmentation of paratime, the waves, the whirlpools, the eddies in space/time that had brought about further fragmentation, further duplication, further multiplication of world after world after world. The Kriths had done a lot of it themselves.

And yet, he realized, as he prepared to move uptime again, some of it was *his own* doing: in going downtime, in challenging the Tromas on KHL-000 in A.D. 1610, he had set into motion still another "new" set of probabilities, more *possible* ways that things *could have been*. In the chronological period A.D. 1610–2500, a vast and still increasing number of possible worlds had come into being, and as each moved forward in time, approached still more possible alternatives, they fragmented further, moving further and still further from probability into improbability, demanding more and more from the substance of space/time, drawing the fabric of the universe thinner and thinner, ever closer to its bursting point.

The fear was still in him as he launched himself uptime again. And as he moved he continued to scan the worlds around him, he found the Lines more and more confused, the fabric of space/time thinner and thinner still. How much more would it take to tear it? he wondered. And what would happen if it tore?—when it tore? What would a hole in the universe, in the universe of the universes, become?

The Tromas had once had an answer to that too, he thought.

He paused again in his movement uptime, and scanned the parallel worlds.

Some calendars would have recorded the date in time as A.D. 1920.

A world here: KHL-000 much as Mathers had known it, a highly civilized world of cities and landscaped parks, of Kriths and their companions; yet, for all that, it was a world over which hung the pall of doom, dark and heavy, eminently menacing.

And beside it in paratime: a blasted, desolate world, created like the moon, seething with radioactivity.

And beside it: a world of men and women huddled in caves, looking with incomprehension at the night sky in which there was no moon, but a series of glittering bands that looked much as the rings of Saturn might look to an observer on that planet.

And beside it: a world where Kriths were the ones who huddled in foul caves, fearful of the sounds in the night, unaware of the powers their ancestors had once possessed.

And beside it: a world dominated by humankind, building a technological culture, a world where airplanes were beginning to take to the sky and iron rails spanned continents, where radio was more than just a curiosity, and where a savage world war loomed on the horizon of history, a war in which biological and chemical weapons might well destroy the human race.

And beside it: a world in which strange, unhuman, unholy figures stalked the forests, alien, asymmetrical things out of nightmares and drug-distorted hallucinations, monstrous things with only the barest glimmerings of intelligence in their grotesque eyes.

And beside it: a world dominated not by humans or by Kriths or by nightmare monsters, but by mammalian humanoids whose skin had a bluish tinge and who had the mastery of a high order of technology, who had craft capable of going to the stars and other craft capable of crossing the Lines of Time . . .

The Shadowy Man felt another chill enter the fear that already filled him. From out of Eric Mathers' memory came these words:

"Their heads and faces were half hidden by transparent helmets, but I saw enough, more than enough: their eyes were too big and their noses too flat and their jaws hinged wrongly and there was an unmistakable tinge of blue to their skin. Oh, they were about the size and shape of men, as far as I could tell from the bulky suits they wore, but there the resemblances ended."

These were the beings whom Mathers had believed to be the founders and the coordinators of the Paratimers, the beings who had called themselves Albigensians when they disguised themselves as humans, the beings who appeared to hate all things human and Krithian and had set out across the Lines, much as had the Kriths, to change the parallel worlds—or to destroy them—to suit their own enigmatic purposes.

But Albert von Heinen, who had worked for them and had once seen them in their natural, undisguised state, had said they came from the far Temporal-West, the products of laboratories, not wombs, artificial beings, androids who had risen to destroy their human masters and then to destroy all humankind on all the Lines. That was what Von Heinen had believed them to be. But . . .

Could it be, the Shadowy Man asked himself, that the Paratimers were not as alien as he had believed? Could it be that they are some variant of the Kriths themselves? Or some alternative race brought into being by the same people who molded the Kriths from human genetic material? Or could they be in a way analogous to the Magers, the companions of the Kriths, some sort of halfway point between human and Krith? Or are they, perhaps, a wild variation of natural evolution, a quantum leap in mutation that created a whole new species on a single, improbable Timeline in this maelstrom of paratemporal madness? Or . . . ?

And if these were the true Albigensians, the true Paratimers, as they certainly appeared to be, then what were they doing exactly here? Had they skudded into this world? Or had they, as he had just speculated, come from this world originally and then gone to the far T-West to begin their work from there?

And how did all this figure into the disruption of the Timelines he was witnessing, the fragmentation of Line after Line after Line into multiplicities of worlds? Were they part of the cause, as he was? Or were they merely an effect of it?

There was too much here for even the Shadowy Man to begin to comprehend at once, though there was an overriding concern in his mind that came back to him, an awareness of the eventual consequences of such universal fragmentation.

He remembered a part of the conversation that Eric Mathers had held with the Tromas. As he again moved uptime toward decision and further action, this came to him:

The Tromas had said: "In the beginning, when the universe came into being, when there was only one master Timeline and it existed in and of itself, it contained in itself all the chronal or parachronal energy, all the temporal potential that would ever exist. Then as the Lines began branching, as the various alternative worlds came into being, that temporal potential began being divided among them."

The Tromas had said: "Each succeeding Timeline, as history progresses, is lower in potential than those which had existed earlier. . . . And . . . the universe *is* limited. Something is either infinite or it is finite. . . . If it is infinite, there is no end *ever*. If it is finite, there is a limit that sooner or later must be reached."

The Tromas had said: "The probability energy, one might say, of the universe is large, large beyond imagining, yet it is not infinite, and for billions of years it has been spreading itself thinner and thinner as more and more Timelines come into being to further subdivide that potential."

Mathers had asked: "Are you saying then that there will come a time when the potential is spread between too many Timelines?"

The Tromas had said: "Exactly, Eric, and when that time comes, the laws of conservation of energy—or something very like them—will come into play to rearrange the probability indices of the Timelines.

"In order to maintain itself—though not exactly in the forms to which we have become accustomed—the universe will have to make major readjustments within itself.

"Timelines vary in their probability. . . . Some are *more likely* than others, more *probable,* and possess, even now, greater values of parachronal energy than do Lines of lesser likelihood.

"Those with lesser likelihood, with lower orders of probability, will *cease to exist,* and their parachronal energy will be redistributed among the Lines of higher orders of probability. That is to say that a vast number of Timelines will cease to exist in order that a smaller number, with greater likelihoods, will be able to continue to exist."

When the universe reordered itself and the lesser Lines ceased to exist, among them would be the Line that had spawned the Kriths, unless they were able to do something to increase their *probability*—which was exactly the purpose of their spreading across the Lines.

But, the Shadowy Man asked himself, were they correct in their projections of when the reordering would come? They had said hundreds or thousands of years uptime. But . . . but did they fully realize how thinly the fabric was already stretched in some areas of space/time? Did they realize how much they themselves had done to weaken the matrix from which *everything* was built?

Farther uptime he moved, crossing the twentieth century and then the twenty-first.

Ultimate questions about the future of all the Timelines would have to wait, he told himself. That was not the immediate problem. The Tromas were. And the problem of *their* existence, and his own, must be settled before he could allow himself the luxury of such metaphysical speculation.

And he thought he now knew where and how he could challenge the Tromas, the time and the place where they would be weak enough, inexperienced enough for him to hope to defeat them—if he had not stretched himself too far when he reached that place in space and time.

That he would see.

Uptime he plunged, into the future far beyond the point where he had come into existence, out into space and far away from the planet called Earth that circled a star called Sol. Into interstellar space . . .

20
UR-427-51-IV

Had an observer been watching the Shadowy Man, had it been possible for human eyes to see him then and to follow the swiftness of his motion in some sort of coherent space/time framework, it would have appeared to the observer that the Shadowy Man moved away from Earth, toward the constellation of Gemini, the Twins.

And had the observer's eyes been able to follow him out of the solar system and into the limitless blackness between the stars, he would have seen the Shadowy Man aiming himself directly toward the second-brightest star in that constellation, Beta Gemini, an orange K0 star that had an absolute magnitude of +0.8, a star somewhat brighter than Earth's Sol, a star often called Pollux on a number of Earths, but known by other names on other worlds, a star listed in the fabled Breston Survey Catalog as UR-427-51.

Had the observer, like the Shadowy Man, been able to step outside the conventionally understood configurations of space and time, had his eyes been able to transcend lightspeed by means of some nonphotonic vision, had he seen by tachyons, perhaps, and had he in this fashion followed the Shadowy Man across the twelve parsecs that separated Sol from Pollux, he would have eventually seen that a host of planets revolved around that orange sun: five of them so-called terrestrial planets, Earthlike in that they were primarily cold balls of stone and perhaps had cores of molten nickel-iron, two of them with gaseous envelopes sufficient to warrant the name "atmosphere." Beyond them, farther out from the star, five more planets revolved on their axes, followed long elliptical orbits around their primary, though these planets were of the type often called "gas giants," worlds not greatly unlike Jupiter or Saturn, though none was as large as Jupiter; in the planetary system of UR-427-51, the total mass of the outer planets was more evenly distributed among the five bodies.

The observer would have seen that the Shadowy Man paid scant attention to the large, gaseous worlds, but swept past them across the plane of the ecliptic and centered his attention on the planet that lay fourth from its sun, a world more distant from Pollux than Earth is from Sol, but at such a distance that it received only a little less heat and light, at least in its upper atmosphere.

The observer would have seen that the nucleus of mental concentration that was the Shadowy Man slowed as he approached UR-427-51-IV, slowed and then swept around it in a great spiraling orbit, examining the planet as the first interstellar probes must have examined it when they discovered the star's planetary system.

The Shadowy Man was in no hurry now, or so he insisted to himself. He must approach slowly, carefully, examining the world below him and determining as much about it as possible before actually pushing his focus of consciousness toward the surface. No hasty rushing in this time. He must be careful; he must be certain, absolutely certain, of everything before he once again challenged the Tromas, or what might now be the proto-Tromas, for as yet he doubted that the Krithian females had full awareness of their potentially enormous power.

In terms of Earth's calendars, one particular calendar that Eric Mathers had often had reference to, it was sometime in the twenty-fourth century, he believed, though he was uncertain of the exact year, perhaps between 2340 and 2350, although the exact year was not a matter of great importance. The Kriths had been here for about a century, genetically modified colonists sprung from human stock, and adapted, by the scientists and technicians of their particular Earth, to survival in the unpleasant environment of the world he saw below him. It would be another fifty or sixty years, as time was measured on Earth, before they would be ready to commandeer a supply ship and in it return to the planet that had created them and then sent them out here.

Now they would be wondering, asking questions, growing within themselves a bitterness toward Earth-norm humans that they would probably never fully express. At least the Kriths had never shown the fullness of their hatred, as far as he knew. But then they had never shown great love toward normal humankind either.

(And what of the blue-skinned ones? he asked himself. If they were akin to the Kriths, if their origin was similar to or identical with that of the Kriths, had they not shown their hatred toward mankind? And he remembered the horrible desolation of world after world among the Albigensian Lines, worlds blasted by thermonuclear hell to lifeless balls of burning stone. Compared to them, the Kriths actually seemed beneficent.)

Around the planet and around again he orbited, each circuit of the planet bringing him closer to the surface. From this distance, UR-427-51-IV was a beautiful world, yet unlike Earth, a dazzling radiance under Pollux, not greatly unlike Venus as seen from a distance, although its cloud cover was less than that of Venus, greater than that of Earth. Beneath those clouds, which did show occasional breaks through which the surface was visible, the greenhouse effect had been at work for long ages, though not with the cataclysmic kind of temperature building Earth's sister world had seen. Enough breaks existed in this cloud cover, sufficient forces were at work to allow at least some of the infrared of the lower atmosphere to leak back into space. Had this not been so, even Kriths could not have survived here. To the best of the Shadowy Man's knowledge, no one on any Line had ever been able to survive unprotected on Venus' surface, no matter how greatly his genes had been modified.

Below the almost but not quite perpetual covering of clouds, the planet was hot, far too hot for Eric Mathers or his kind to have endured for long without extensive refrigeration and air-conditioning facilities. Kriths, or the proto-Kriths who dwelt there now, could endure it, though they might not have found it the most pleasant of climates.

It was a world with an axial tilt greater than Earth's, a world where winds of high velocity swept through the atmosphere, where great storms boiled, where thunder played a nearly continual tune and lightning frequently illuminated the underside of the dark, heavy clouds. It was a world where rain fell as often as it did not, where great oceans spread across most of the surface, untroubled by lunar tides, churned only by the pull of Pollux and its companion planets and by the frequent storms that lashed across uncounted leagues of water. Where there was land on UR-427-51-IV, it was mostly swamp, forever wet to a greater or lesser degre, for whatever volcanism the planet had, whatever slipping continental plates might have crushed together, whatever mountain ranges might once have reared toward the dark skies, constant rain and wind had quickly eroded them, tumbling stone and earth and mud back into the sea from which they had come.

It was not a pleasant world, either to the humans who had discovered it and its potential value or to the colonists they had adapted from their own flesh and blood, their own fertilized ova, to dwell here, doing tasks that unmodified men and women of Earth did not wish to do. It had been largely a cold, economic decision, he suspected, to send genetically modified colonists here rather than send unmodified Earth-norms who would have required elaborate life-support systems, complex protection from the environment, insulated, bubble-enclosed housing, and much more. It was simply cheaper to send the genetically modified, who could get by without these things.

The Shadowy Man moved still closer to the surface, noting in his passage the observation satellites strung across the skies, satellites with electronic eyes, with cameras and antennae that constantly watched the turning world below.

And he noted the single inhabited platform that circled the world in a polar orbit. Not a large station by any means, but sufficient to hold four Earth-norm humans in some degree of comfort and safety. It was the four inhabitants of this platform who monitored the world of the colonists below, who directed their tasks, who sent down to the planet robotic cargo shuttles to carry supplies to the colonists, matériel essential to their survival that they could not produce themselves, and to carry back into orbit for transshipment to Earth the results of the colonists' labor: a particular and rather esoteric drug manufactured by a plant that grew in the shallow swamps; the lovely, multicolored fur of a near-mammal that looked something like an otter and something like a cat, but differed from both; the beautiful gemlike stones created inside the bodies of certain deep-sea crustaceans, amphibious creatures that returned to the shore annually to breed, and to be captured by the colonists.

While still outside of all but the most rarefied portions of the atmosphere, the Shadowy Man began to probe into the psionic world, into the darkness that was something other than the absence of light, the absence, rather, of intellect, and within that darkness began to search out the bright points of consciousness, of self-awareness.

On the surface of the planet below he found those points of light, a familiar kind of mind now, the Krithian mind. He found clusters of these lights, apparently strung out along an archipelago, clusters that in most cases consisted of no more than a few dozen individuals each, though toward the center of the curved line they formed was a larger cluster, and within that cluster was a group of ten minds that glowed more brightly than the others, that were more aware, more powerful, that reinforced one another through psionic interchange, through something that might have been called resonance but was not quite the same as that.

In their total, the Shadowy Man thought as he lowered his focus of consciousness still closer to the surface, as he withdrew his probes so that the ones below would not yet become aware of his presence, there were no more than a few hundred of the colonists, and knowing what great handicaps had been placed on their reproduction, he wondered how it would be possible for so small a group to survive even the next fifty or sixty years, much less commandeer a spaceship to carry them to Earth. But they would do that, both survive and eventually leave this world, he was certain. The histories of hundreds of Timelines bore ample witness to that.

With electromagnetic vision but remotely akin to human sight, the Shadowy Man looked as he lowered himself through the perpetual overcast and saw below him the dark world under the clouds, saw the wind-whipped rain charging in near-torrents across the far southern archipelago, as thunder rolled across the sky and great bolts of lethal lightning crackled between the clouds and the stunted growths of trees that huddled close to the damp land.

On one of those islands, amid a cluster of supple reeds that bent with the force of the wind, a dozen or more naked Kriths, bigger and physically stronger than most men, were struggling in the downpour to draw in a net that contained a score or more large crustaceans, lobsterlike animals with bulging eyes and long, dangerous-looking pincers that snapped at the ropes that held them and at the fingers that held the ropes. More than one of the Kriths was missing a finger or two from each of his hands.

As the Shadowy Man watched, one of the struggling Kriths lost his footing on the muddy soil as he tugged at the net, stumbled, fell, then slid, foundering into the water, flailing about with his arms and prehensile tail, to no avail. His companions saw what had happened, but none of them dared release his grip on the net. The struggle was already so awkwardly balanced that the loss of another pair of hands would have certainly meant the loss of the net and its contents. They fought to pull the net from the water, perhaps hoping their companion could regain land without their help.

The Krith who had fallen into the water surfaced, gasped for air, and fought to stay afloat. He did not cry out for help. He seemed to know that his companions would help him if they could, but now could not. For a few moments he seemed to have gained some control over the situation. It appeared that he might be able to make his way back to land without help. But that changed in moments. As he half swam, half crawled toward the higher ground, an expression of astonishment, then pain, crossed his flat features. He flailed again and fell backward, the water around him turning to a muddy crimson. He screamed, again screamed, again struggled awkwardly toward land.

Now the other Kriths had managed to conquer the struggling crustaceans within the net, exerted an enormous final effort, and drew the net from the water onto the soggy land. While three of them hurried to secure the net to pegs driven into the ground and hold the crustaceans within their fibrous prison, the others dashed back to the edge of the water, formed a living ladder of themselves, moved toward the weakening, wounded Krith, touched hands with him, and pulled him to safety.

When at last they had him out of the water and he lay on the damp earth, gasping for air, sobbing in pain, the Shadowy Man could see what had happened. Teeth or pincers, claws or tentacles, he could not tell which, had fastened onto the Krith, had torn away most of his tail, the toes and most of the flesh of one foot, strips of flesh from both calves and thighs, and had left his genitals an unrecognizable mass of mangled flesh. He probably would live, had not poison been introduced into his system, did not infection enter the wounds. But whether he would wish to live in such a fashion was another question.

There was perhaps in the Shadowy Man a new understanding, a new appreciation of the Kriths, as he moved his consciousness away from that spot. It had not been easy, nor had it been pleasant, that first century or two of their racial existence. Mere survival had been a hard-won prize. And along with that understanding there came to him a glimmering of admiration. Under such conditions could another sapient race have survived at all? Could humankind have done as well as the Kriths had?

Above the islands he moved again, across them, toward the center of the long, slightly curving archipelago, toward the place where he had detected the largest cluster of minds, where he had detected the brighter points of psionic light, the more intense concentrations of mind that were the Tromas, or the proto-Tromas, the ten females of the race. And he asked himself: With such attrition as I have just seen, how can *they* even maintain the race, much less increase it?

One of the islands jutted a little higher above the level of the sea, provided a greater slope for the runoff of rain water, and was a bit dryer than the other islands. And on the highest point of the curving, dome-like island stood a cluster of rude huts, jerry-built affairs of reeds and vines, thatched with the broad leaves of some low-growing plant, huts without windows, but with doors covered with the colorful hides of some semiaquatic mammal-like creatures.

At first sight there was no indication that these people were the product and the agents of a civilization with the capability of crossing twelve parsecs of space in huge, plasma-powered spaceships. But on closer examination, in the center of the cluster of huts there stood something that could have come only from a highly advanced technology. A metal cylinder just slightly taller than the largest of the huts, of gleaming metal and glass that would have sparkled brightly had there been sunlight rather than this perpetual gloom, that did reflect brilliantly the flashes of lightning across the sky, an artifact from distant Earth that could have been nothing less than a communications center, a radio/video/laser transceiver of great power, a holographic tank that would display images sent down from the orbiting platform, from the overseers who commanded from many miles above in the comparative safety of their metal cocoon.

Not far from the cluster of huts was a cleared area where the dirt had been packed firmly, then covered with broken bits of stone and shell, obviously the landing field for the cargo shuttles that passed between the islands and the orbiting platform. But it was not the landing field that attracted the Shadowy Man's attention.

Rather, it was the largest of the huts, the one nearest the communications cylinder. Even without probing, he was aware that in that hut dwelt the females of the race, who had already, even this early in their history, become the directors of the actions of the proto-Kriths, the givers of wisdom, and who might now have some glimmerings of tomorrow and the awesome powers they and their people would one day wield. . . .

Would wield, unless the Shadowy Man could stop them now.

Now he paused, hovered, analyzed. He was far, far from home, in frames of reference that encompassed space and time and paratime. The nexus that connected him with his corporeal bodies was now a tenuous one, stretched across great five-dimensional distances. And he was aware of the lessening of his powers, of how far across the continuua he would have to draw the forces with which he was to do battle.

Yet, he was not pitting his strength against the Tromas of KHL-000 on their own world, their own time, with centuries of experience behind them. He was pitting himself against ten tired female Kriths who huddled in a rain-drenched hut, who had never had enough to eat, who had never received proper care or medical attention, who were lashed by weather and heat and parasites, who did not yet fully comprehend the potentials within themselves.

He could defeat *them*.

Couldn't he?

And as he took a brief glance at them, as he flashed his electromagnetic vision into and then out of the hut, as he saw them huddling in the semidarkness of the hut's interior, illuminated feebly by two sputtering oil lamps, he felt a great sense of pity, of sympathy, even of concern for their wretched condition. Could he bring himself to strike against *them*, these pitiful half-humans who had been born to suffer and to die as lonely, hopeless castaways over 19×10^{12} miles from the homeworld Earth?

Yes, he could.

Now they were exactly as he saw them. But . . . looking across time and space and paratime, he saw other things through the vision of Eric Mathers' memory: he saw the vast armies of Timeliners moving from parallel Earth to parallel Earth to alter the histories of uncounted worlds in accordance with a plan the Tromas had developed in order to increase *their* chances of survival, heedless of what their meddling might do to millions upon millions of innocent human beings; he saw wars and death and destruction; he saw the deaths of a girl named Kristin and of a girl named Marissa, of a man named Hillary Tracy and a man named Jock Kouzenzas, of the men and women of New Anglia, and of so many, many others that he could not distinguish all of them; he saw the dark-uniformed bodyguards of the Kriths, men like Pall and Marth, no longer human except in their bodily forms, more Krith than man in their minds; he saw armies of the Mager-types, the Companions, who were not men at all but something the Kriths themselves had created or had had created for them; he saw all the lies and deceptions that the Kriths had perpetrated over the years; and most of all he saw the Tromas in their "palace" on KHL-000 and sensed the power they possessed and would use to destroy the Shadowy Man and anyone else who stood between them and the future as they envisioned it, a future that, when the universe had reordered itself toward greater simplicity, would have the Kriths supreme on all the Lines of Time.

Yes, he would do it. He would attack and destroy these pitiful wretches. He had no other choice if man was ever to be free of them and be allowed to seek his own multiple destinies across the Lines of Time.

From remote distances across time and space he drew toward him energies, forces, powers, shaped them into lances of fire and spears of fury. He drew them back, tensed, and then for a moment, before he launched his attack, he projected out of the sky and into the hut this mental construction:

If you can see into tomorrow, you will know who I

*am and why I have come. I do not do this for pleasure,
but because it must be done. . . .*

And he was briefly aware of their astonishment,
their fear.

Then his probe was gone, his shields were up, and
toward and into the hut he hurled his psionic blasts.

The inside of the hut shimmered with auroral brightness, sparks and streams of lightning flickered across
the interior walls, the dryer reeds inside smoldering
and then beginning to burn. The ten females of the
proto-Tromas writhed in agony, curled into balls, tumbled grotesquely across the floor, screaming in pain
and terror.

For an instant he lowered his shield and peered into
the hut.

Sisters . . . A mental voice was crying out of its
pain. *Sisters, rally to me, to me. . . .*

Incoherent mentations. Pain climbing toward the sky.
One figure ceasing its horrible writhing, falling still,
silent, the brightness of its mind fading to blackness,
nothingness, death.

*Sisters, he has come. Rally to me. We can still fight
back. . . .*

Nine consciousnesses now, through their pain seeking one another, converging, melting, blending, becoming one.

The Shadowy Man reached out into space/time, a
minor sensation of triumph in him. He had killed one
of them; their collective strength would not be as
great as it could have been. Their collective strength
was . . .

Now, sisters! . . .

As he gathered new energies into himself, as he
forged new weapons to dash against them, the females
as a single entity struck, battered against his not fully
sustained shields, broke through them, hurled him backward.

Damn you! he cried to himself, now feeling pain as

they did, pushing away their force, bringing his shields back up, completing the manufacture of his weapons, deploying them, using them.

The invisible shields of the females shimmered with furious incandescence. Around them, the walls of the hut began to catch fire.

Outside, the male Kriths of the village, who had some awareness of what was happening, rushed to offer what help they could to their females, their guardians.

Tear down the walls, brothers/husbands, they cried. *Keep the fire away from us.* . . . Out of their pain and their fury they screamed.

With bare hands, two dozen or so male Kriths attacked the burning hut, ripped away portions of it, threw them across the damp earth, and let the rain do its work.

The females were hurt, were in pain both psionic and physical, for the males had not acted quickly enough, despite their swiftness, and the flames had licked across them, embers had scorched their flesh. But still they had repelled the blasts he had thrown at them, had held their shields.

Damn you! the Shadowy Man said to himself again, throwing up his own shields to ward off the flames and fury they cast at him. Now the pity and the sympathy were gone from him; now there was only his own fury and a desire to destroy them.

Again he reached out, again sought raw energy from which to build more weapons, groped across darkness, found . . . found dwindling supplies. He was too far away. Too far. And the females were rallying again.

Know this, thou force from out of time . . . they cried at him. *Know this: you cannot now defeat us, now or ever. Have done with it. Let us be.* . . .

What energy he could he took and brought it to this place, molding it, shaping it, propelling it against the shields of the females, which again flickered and burned brightly. Once again they held off the bulk of his attack, swept it away, felt only minor pain. The nine of them still held, and prepared to lunge against him.

The Shadowy Man sought to strengthen his shields once more, found them weaker still and weakening more. His reserves were almost gone. Across the light-years, across the centuries, he tried to drag replacement powers, reinforcement energies, but the gulf was too great, too great.

Again the Krithian females struck against him, battering his shields again and again, smashing through them, tearing them down one after the other, forcing piercing lances of psionic force through them and into him.

The Shadowy Man screamed, felt the last of his defenses fall, felt himself being rocked backward in space, in time.

No, damn you, no! he cried silently, but that was all he could do. They had defeated him again. Before they could strike against him once more, before they could drive more bolts of hellish fury into him and through him across time and space into the bodies that were his component parts, he disengaged, withdrew, fled, hung suspended Nowhere, Nowhen.

They had beaten him. And they had been right: *You cannot now defeat us, now or ever. . . .*

He had lost again.

Perhaps for the last time.

21
The Sundering of Time

Still feeling the agony inflicted upon him by the blows of the proto-Tromas, still tasting in his mind the gall of defeat, the Shadowy Man slowly propelled the focus of his consciousness backward through time, across space and across paratime toward the physical bodies in the Underground of the BrathelLanza. Along with the pain there was confusion and a sense of hopelessness.

He had done what he had been able to do. There seemed no other avenues to pursue. Even in their infancy the Tromas were more than a match for him. And although he thought that he could have beaten them had he not been so thinly drawn, he knew that to be only academic. The facts being what they were, there was no way he could hope ever to meet the Tromas with an advantage over them. Perhaps there was, after all, a measure of predestination in the universe; perhaps it had been preordained that the Kriths would dominate all the Lines of Time, the bastard children of humankind, perhaps, but better suited for rule of the continuua of Earths.

So, despite his efforts, by and large the future would be as the Tromas had always seen it. When finally, centuries hence, the Timelines had multiplied so greatly that the universe would be forced to reorder itself to greater simplicity, the Kriths would most likely have had ample opportunity to assure their continued existence after that reordering. Then what? Once they had accomplished their racial goal, what would they do next?

The Kriths had no great love for their parent race, humankind, he knew, and would probably feel no significant obligation toward whatever portion of that race still existed after the reordering, whatever human Lines still remained, which should be a considerable number, considering the vast number of Lines spawned by mankind's decisions when facing Either-Or. Would the Kriths finally take their vengeance on the race that had created them and then sent them off to the living hell of UR-427-51-IV? Or would they by then have gained sufficient insight to no longer hate humankind for being what it was? Would they allow the race of Eric Mathers and his kind to go on living, developing, perhaps to one day live up to the standards it sometimes tried to set for itself but seldom met? If the Kriths did let humankind go on, then in what status? As slaves of the Kriths? As inferior people to do their bidding, to further advance the Kriths and further assure *their* continued survival during any future universal catastrophe? He did not know, could only speculate, but there was still enough of the human in him, enough of Eric Mathers, for him to feel a great concern, a fear for the future of man.

But what could he do?

He drifted back in space and time and paratime toward the Underground and the place of his physical existence as the senior of his resonating replicates. Now he could not even assure the survival of the physical body of Eric Mathers, though perhaps something could be done to help him. Perhaps.

As he came closer in space/time, as he moved through the nothingness that is everything, new perceptions came to him, sensations that impinged on his withdrawn consciousness. He looked out of himself, felt, probed, sensed.

Downtime, he thought, downtime there is *something*. What, he could not have said, could not have even guessed, but he was aware of something that had happened/was happening/would happen, something that did have/was having/would have great consequences for all the Lines of Time.

With a growing sense of anxiety, forgetting momentarily the pain and humiliation, he thrust himself through nothingness with greater force, swept downtime toward the space/time of Eric Mathers and the replicates, then past them and farther into the "past."

Then he saw, felt knew. . . .

He had encountered it before, but then it had been farther downtime, more remote in the chronological past as Eric Mathers would have conceived it. And *it* moved. . . .

A great wavefront was coming uptime, sweeping forward, fracturing and sundering as it came, spawning world after world after world, an ever-growing multiplicity of Timelines. The meddling of the Tromas, their flitting through and past themselves in retrograde time, their being/not being in duplication of themselves in the same relative space/time—all this, multiplied by the activities of the Shadowy Man in his own movements through time and his added manipulation of spatio-temporal events, had brought into being this *something* that was the wavefront, *something* that was a swelling tide of rupturing paratime, duplicated, quadrupled world after world: worlds twinned, spawned, modified, and mutated, spreading the fabric of all the universes, all the continuua, thinner, thinner, ever thinner. . . .

And in the midst of this wavefront, spreading like a second cancer across the multiplicity of worlds, were the bluish-tinted creatures who were the true Paratimers, the beings truly behind Staunton and the raid on Fort Lothairin and who, perhaps, had been behind the destruction of the BrathelLanza, the nonhumans, non-Kriths who were the actual operating force behind so much that had been done in opposition to the Kriths—and in opposition to mankind as well.

Like the Kriths, the Paratimers sought to subvert a vast number of Earths, to bring them under their control, to alter the master plans of the Kriths and create futures more to their own liking.

But why? the Shadowy Man wondered. And what are they?

As he moved backward in chronological time, the Shadowy Man paused only briefly, snatching an image here, another image there, putting together in his composite mind a backward-running motion picture film that led him to the devastated Albigensian Lines of the far Temporal-West, to the dead, blasted worlds Eric Mathers and Sally had found when they had fled from Kar-hinter and sought Mica's world. Still farther back in chronotime: balls of thermonuclear flame and towering mushrooms of dark smoke; missiles climbing on tails of fire from hidden silos, from submerged submarines, falling from orbiting stations: a war that spanned a dozen parallel Earths and more, a war fought by the Kriths and their human servants who weren't yet Timeliners against the Paratimers.

Kriths! the Shadowy Man wondered. On worlds this far to the T-West? But the Kriths had never come this far to the T-West, had they? But perhaps they had. Perhaps they had—originally.

Still farther back in time: the Kriths consolidating their hold on a world, a single world; Kriths without their Great Lies and their Timeliner mercenaries and their vast propaganda machines to convince humans of their beneficence; Kriths who had established a tyrannical rule over the race who had created them and sent them to a hell among the stars; a beleaguered humanity fighting a losing war against its creation, then turning to fight with fire, unleashing against the Kriths a second subspecies created in the laboratories of genetic engineers, a second subspecies as different from the Kriths as the Kriths were different from their ancestral humans, a second subspecies that turned against its embattled creators and destroyed them before taking up the war against the Kriths and their human servants.

Insanity! the Shadowy Man cried within himself. And wondered if any of what he was witnessing had any reality at all or was just some vague, fanciful twist of probability/improbability as the universe of universes grew near sundering, as the maddened wavefront swept uptime, spawning a phantasmagoria of worlds and drawing thinner yet the fabric of totality.

He looked again at the wavefront that moved forward in chronological time and thought: in such a condition the universe cannot long endure. If the wavefront were to spread much farther uptime, increasing the number of existing Lines by exponential powers, the universe would have to crumble to its very foundations, or reorder itself.

The concept of godhead, of deity, had little place in his mind, in his thoughts, as he considered the restructuring of the universe to greater simplicity. Yet there was about it, almost, the feeling of a directing intelligence, a guiding force that would see to it that the universe remained intact, did not crumble into an infinite number of bright but meaningless fragments. Something, mind or force or basic structure, would not let this happen, would step in and see to it that the now almost incoherent multiplicity was reordered into sanity and greater simplicity. What it was even the Shadowy Man did not know. He did not call it God, though perhaps that name could have been applied. Whatever the name, he knew *it* was there and *it* would act. Soon. Very soon.

The Tromas had been right in their judgment of the coming necessity of universal reorganization. But their time scale had been off, very far off. Not hundreds or thousands of years from the moment Eric Mathers stood in the palace of the Tromas and learned of it from them, but only months ahead in time.

But then they couldn't have known all that the

Shadowy Man now knew, couldn't have foreseen it, could they?

There was a great deal more he knew now, and he realized that the Tromas had not even begun to fully understand the nature of time, nor had he. Perhaps it was incomprehensible. Perhaps it did take a universal godhead to fully comprehend what time was/is/will be, how it is an aspect of the same thing of which paratime is an aspect, of which all energy and matter too are aspects.

As wrong as was the viewpoint of time being a linearly progressing thing, so was it equally wrong to consider time an all-existing thing, the future, the present, and the past already in final shape and unchangeable. Time was not such a simple thing. It was far more complex than that—or perhaps far less so: or both at once. And it existed not by the rules laid down by men or Kriths or any other finite intelligences. It, and all the universe, existed by its own rules, regardless of whether anyone knew those rules.

What the Tromas had told Eric Mathers about the nature of time had not been *wrong*, no more than Newtonian physics were *wrong*. Just incomplete. If he carried the analogy forward: his present knowledge of time was Einsteinian to their Newtonian, and just as Einstein had superseded Newton, had explained more of the workings of the universe, so too had his viewpoint been incomplete and would one day be replaced by another viewpoint that more nearly comprehended it all.

How ignorant we will always be! he said to himself. And "looked" at the wavefront that swept glittering and screaming uptime, the wavefront that he had abetted. Unwittingly, unknowingly, by means he had not intentionally devised, but because of what he had done, the sundering of the universe would come long before the Kriths were ready for it, long before they had become so entrenched in the Timelines that nothing could dislodge them. They had greatly increased their probability, of course. But not enough. Though they commanded hundreds of Timelines, there were millions more they had not touched, and for each they had touched, for each Line they had manipulated and altered, there stood beside it its parallel, which they had not touched, perhaps could not touch, for by their very touching of a Line they engendered its alternative, a Line they had not influenced. Had they realized this? That their very manipulation, too, had twinned each Line they had reached, had created its duplicate—one world manipulated, one not—so that no matter how many worlds they entered, altered, they could never hope to encompass even a small fraction of all the Lines of Time, Lines they themselves helped to multiply at an ever-increasing rate. Would they ever have been able to keep up with it?

Did it matter now? he asked himself, pausing in space/time, observing the wavefront that "moved forward" at a rate of its own, creating a subtime within the totality of time.

When the universal catastrophe came, when the majority of Timelines with lower orders of probability winked out of existence, *would never have been*, so too would the Kriths cease to exist, so too would they never have been. Neither they nor the Paratimers, whatever they were, nor all the works they had set out to do would ever have existed.

He watched the wavefront, calculated, saw the coming of the limits, the final sundering when catastrophe would occur.

He fixed a date in his mind. The year A.D. 1973 as the calendar was reckoned on the world of Sally's birth. Early in the year. What day? The sixty-third day of that year. The month of March. The fourth day of that month, on Sally's calendar.

Then it would be over. All of it. No more Kriths. No more Timeliners. No more Paratimers.

He had won; in a very real sense he had accomplished what he had set out to do. . . .

And what of himself?

He too was a creature of the Kriths—Eric Mathers was a creature of the Kriths, so thus was he. And so was Sally. So were . . .

Amid the numbness that spread across his consciousness, amid the questions and the fear, there came another realization. . . .

He himself had come/would come into being on 4 March 1973. Before that there had been no Shadowy Man.

Then . . . did he/would he exist?

Feeling a terror that could only be called mortal, the Shadowy Man hurled himself through nothingness, uptime, toward the Underground and the immobile body of Eric Mathers, the motionless replicates, his very existence. . . .

22
The Last Encounter

Once more the Underground of the BrathelLanza enveloped the Shadowy Man. He settled into the individual bodies and into the resonance patterns that existed among those bodies, feeling almost as a human might feel, returning to the comfort and security of his mother's womb, for this was the womb from which the Shadowy Man had been born.

The sense of terror partially slipped from him, receding from the front of his consciousness, although he did not forget that the end was approaching—the end of the universe as he had known it, the end of the Kriths and the Timeliners and all the things they had done, and the end of the mysterious Paratimers and their efforts across the Lines. How soon, he did not know. Now? An hour from now? Anytime . . . He could not calculate the time of sundering with that precision; yet, within the next six to eight hours at the most, he thought.

And still there were things he had to do, things that might be totally futile now, but he must make every effort to complete the past as Eric Mathers had experienced it—if he did not, he suddenly asked himself, how would that affect things? If the universal reorganization came before he had completed his work, what would that do to his participation in the chronological past? Wipe it out? Alter things in the Kriths' favor? Paradoxes . . .

He was not certain of any of this, but he could take no chances. He knew that he must complete Eric Mathers' experiences, down to the last detail he could

cull from his memory, and then—if at all possible—
make some provisions for the continued existence of
Eric Mathers, should he still exist after the reordering
of the universe. The continuation of his own existence,
that of himself as the Shadowy Man, he knew to be
considerably unlikely. But if he could save at least the
Eric Mathers portion of himself, that would be enough.
If the universe didn't destroy *him* . . .

Once again he looked out through the eyes of
Mathers and saw the chronometer in the recording
room. More time had gone by, to the motionless figure
strapped in the chair—over an hour since he had last
looked out through those eyes. The chronometer read
13:50:17. Early afternoon. Perhaps the universe still
had a few hours before it altered itself, before the
parachronal subtime wavefront swept this far uptime
and demanded that the universe reorder itself toward
greater simplicity, or cease to exist altogether.

A few hours, perhaps . . .

Now, he told himself, there are three things I must
do.

First: he must provide for the "parachronal convolution" through which Eric Mathers and Sally had
escaped KHL-000, the sphere of blackness that had
awaited them on the roof of the apartment building
toward which they had fled as the Shadowy Man bat-
tled the Tromas in their own place/time, the first and
perhaps the worst of his encounters with the Krithian
females. While Mathers was under attack by the
Tromas, after the Shadowy Man's defeat by them, Sally
had dragged him into the black sphere and through
it they had plunged across space and time, to the
Far World where they had lived for some time, where
Sally still lived on 4 March 1973, and from which
Mathers had begun the adventures, some eleven months
before, that had led him to the Underground of the
BrathelLanza and to evolution into the Shadowy Man.

Mathers and Sally had been told that they had

passed through a "parachronal convolution," a term that had meant nothing to them, though now the Shadowy Man was beginning to have some inkling of what it might be.

Second: he must provide them with a skudder at their destination. It had been there and the Shadowy Man had provided it. So he must now do it; otherwise Mathers could never have left the Far World and come across the Lines to this place that the Shadowy Man presently occupied.

And finally: he must provide for the escape of the corporeal body of Eric Mathers, get him out of this place and into another, safer one; a place where he *might* survive the reordering, if it was possible for him to survive, if it was possible for him to *exist* once the Kriths no longer existed anywhere, on any Line.

Once more the Shadowy Man set out on quest, and in learning how to accomplish the first of his objectives he learned how to accomplish the others.

Time was lost, time that he could not regain, for, as he had suspected, he found that he could not return to the Underground in a time/place he already had occupied. But as time was lost, knowledge was gained.

The composite mind of the senior and his replicates swept back and forth across time and space, searching out bits and pieces of knowledge that the Shadowy Man was now capable of using, always terribly aware that he was in the moments of time just before the reordering of the universe.

He found: esoteric bits of knowledge; fragments of theories about the nature of space/time; ways of manipulating the unraveling of fabric of the universe; means of twisting that fabric into unusual and intricate shapes; processes through which one segment of space/time/paratime could be linked with another, momentarily, tenuously, but sufficiently for a material object to pass from one point to another in the five-sided references; learned how to bring into being a parachronal convolution, a tunnel through time and space and paratime.

He was astonished by the powers he found he could use, and wished that he had learned these tricks earlier, or that the universe would give him more time to fully exploit their value. But now there was a linear progression of subtime, or perhaps a paralinear progression of subtime—the holocaust of the moving wavefront sweeping uptime—that even he could do nothing to alter. He was caught in subtime as fully as any man had ever been caught in the inexorable movement of time in the conventional universe. He could not hold back the hands of *that* clock.

But he could at least do what he had set out to do.

Returning briefly to the Underground, he rested, went over what he had just learned, then launched himself outward again, backward in chronological time and across paratime to the world of the Kriths, KHL-000, A.D. February 1972.

For a moment he poised his consciousness above the top of the apartment building that he had visited before. It was night Here and Now, and from the top of the spire the lights of the vast capital city of the Kriths spread out below him toward the horizon on one side, the dark sea on the other. In the building below, from the open doorway at the top of the stair-well, he could already hear gunfire and the yells of the Mager-guards who pursued Mathers and Sally as they made their attempt to escape. Farther below, in the apartment Sally had occupied, a great struggle had just terminated. His previous self, an earlier Shadowy Man, had just been vanquished by the Tromas and had fled, screaming in pain, back toward the Underground. For a few moments the Tromas would be occupied with their own problems, assessing their victory, seeing to their own minor psionic wounds. If he acted quickly enough, they would never become aware of him. He thought they would not recognize the parachronal convolution for what it was, even if they were to notice it. He hoped.

Mathers and Sally, naked but not unarmed, firing behind them as they came, were about to reach the top of the stairs.

There was no more time for thought. With mental probes, with Waldos of psionic force, he reached out and grabbed a piece of the space/time stuff of Here and Now, held it in an unrelenting grasp; and then, with all the force he could muster, he tore a strand loose and withdrew with it across time and space and paratime, drawing the strand with him.

This is how it works, isn't it? he asked himself, and thought that it was.

Pulling a dimple of time/space/paratime deeper and deeper into nothingness, he drew it toward and finally to his destination, a few weeks downtime, a very short distance relative to spatial distances, but a long, long way across the dimension he called paratime.

There! He had reached it, pulled another pucker out of another world's framework, connected them together.

How long the connection would hold, in terms of chronological time, he did not know. Not long. Minutes at the most. But time enough. Mathers and Sally would see the blackness that the convolution presented to their senses, would realize it to be their means of escape, and, in desperation, would use it. Through it they would pass across to the Far World and there they would be safe. From there Mathers would later follow the path that led him, eventually, to the BrathelLanza and their underground laboratories.

Accomplished! he said to himself, a sense of relief coming over him. He had done this much. He could do the rest. And he could hope that in the end it all would have meant something.

Pausing only momentarily, he then moved to accomplish the second of his three objectives. Once again he propelled himself into the future, leaped a few Lines horizontally in paratime until he located a world where the Kriths and the Timeliners had established themselves, searched for a skudder pool or its equivalent on that world, and found one.

The year was A.D. 2004, as chronological time is measured, a few miles from a place occupied by Atlanta, Georgia, on some worlds, where the Timeliners had set up a large, well-equipped base. Into this base the Shadowy Man went, to a large depot building that contained nearly a score of brand-new skudders, just recently arrived there from the Line of their manufacture. Blue-clad Timeliner technicians were completing their final checks of the craft before sending them out into the field. One of these skudders would do perfectly for Mathers' future needs.

The Shadowy Man was feeling almost happy as he moved into the fabric of space/time around one of the new skudders, as he extended psionic appendages to grasp that fabric. The fact that this was a "future" world that would soon cease to exist, with the coming of the universal reorganization, did not bother him in the least; in fact, there seemed to be something very funny about it. As long as the skudder stayed downtime of 4 March 1973, it would have *some* probability— enough, at least, to serve his purposes and Mathers'.

And there was something very funny about the expressions on the faces of the technicians as the skudder vanished before their eyes, as the depot reverberated with the sound of imploding air, rushing in to fill the vacuum left by the skudder's sudden and unexpected departure.

With the skudder nestled in a capsule of detached space/time, the Shadowy Man drew it across nothingness until he reached the Far World again and completed the convolution. The skudder then sat but a short distance from where Mathers and Sally would come out of their escape route.

There was a feeling within him that would have been a smile on a human face, a satisfaction with this stage of his work, when the Shadowy Man retreated back to the Underground for what he anticipated to be the next to last time, back to where he could check the passage of chronological time as seen by Eric Mathers and decide how to go about the last, final phase of his labors.

He was astonished at what he found there, though he knew he should not have been. He should have anticipated it. For all the vast mental powers he had, he knew that he was but an infant in his knowledge of their use. And it was very unlikely that he would be given the opportunity to complete his maturation.

Eric Mathers and the replicates were no longer alone in the Underground. People had entered, more than one kind of *people*. . . .

Through the eyes of Mathers the Shadowy Man looked, and with Mathers' ears he heard.

There was the sound of several pairs of feet moving in the corridor outside the recording room, and distant voices speaking a language Eric Mathers had heard before, a variation of Middle French as spoken by the so-called Albigensian Paratimers, male voices and female voices he soon recognized. One of those voices—one he had heard quite recently—was saying, as its owner approached the door of the recording room:

"In all likelihood, Scoti, he was in one of the mnemonic-recording rooms when the raid took place. If that is so, he may well still be in one of them, and alive. At least the police do not have him, and his body does not appear to be among the dead. I'm certain no one escaped."

"You said he might be under the influence of drugs, OrDjina," said a voice that Eric Mathers hadn't heard in quite some time, the voice of a man named Scoti Hauser Angelus, who had been the second in command of the Paratimers, Mica's lieutenant, in the place called Staunton.

"Yes, that's so," replied the lady OrDjina. "That must somehow be related to the phenomenon you described."

"That may well be," said the voice of another woman, a voice that was in Mathers' memory as well.

"Here," said OrDjina's voice. "This door does not appear to have been opened."

The Shadowy Man tensed, waited, listened, as a hand curled around the knob of the door, turned the knob, and tried to force open the bolted door.

"It's locked," said Scoti's voice. "That figures."

"Then kick it open," said a voice that the Shadowy Man did not recognize, a voice with an accent unknown to Eric Mathers, a voice that somehow did not sound like that of a human.

"Right," replied Scoti's voice; then he grunted as he kicked the door, rattling it and the wall.

"Kick it again," said the alien voice.

"Right," Scoti repeated, and once more the Paratimer kicked savagely at the door. This time there came with it the sound of wood splintering.

"Once more," said the voice that the Shadowy Man did not believe to come from a human mouth and throat.

With the third kick the lock broke and the door swung inward.

There were six individuals in the corridor, six who began to come into the room to look down at the unmoving form of Eric Mathers.

The first of these was the lady OrDjina, dressed in a black, tight-fitting gown more appropriate for a dinner party than for the charnel house that the Underground had become. There was an ugly pistol in her hand, and on her face a look of satisfaction, an expression that briefly turned to one of disgust when she saw the mutilated body of the technician MaLarba on the floor near Mathers' chair. Her eyes quickly went back to the figure in the chair and the look of satisfaction returned.

Immediately behind her was a stocky, dusky-skinned man, fairer than OrDjina, a man whom Mathers had once considered an improbable blend of Italian and Nipponese parentage. Scoti, also armed, was dressed in a blouse and slacks of pale green, and had a look of satisfaction similar to that of OrDjina's—a look that swept the gamut from revulsion, when he saw MaLarba's body, to astonishment, when he saw the face of the man in the chair before him, and finally to triumph.

"My God, OrDjina!" He gasped, glanced back at the others behind him for confirmation, then continued: "Do you know who your HarkosNor *really* is?"

"No. Should I?" OrDjina asked, puzzled.

Scoti laughed, then clenched his left fist and shook it toward the man strapped in the chair. "Dammit, we should have known who he was."

"This does sort of tie things together, doesn't it?" said a young, beautiful, black-skinned woman, who was the third to enter the room, and who was dressed similarly to Scoti, and armed as he was. Long, tempestuous nights with G'lendal came up out of Mathers' memory. She would have been difficult to forget.

"Oh, doesn't it!" Scoti gloated. "All of it begins to make sense now."

"Well, who is he?" OrDjina demanded.

Before Scoti could answer, the remaining three had filed into the room. Two of them, a black man and woman, were dressed in the long white robes of Paratimer physicians, with the badges of telepaths on their chests. As they came into the room, each was moving exactly as the other did, down to the most subtle gestures. The Shadowy Man knew who they were, something of a forerunner of himself: Sol-Jodala they/

it were called. And were probably among the finest, most talented physicians in all the universes.

The sixth individual gave the Shadowy Man pause as he—a male, surely—moved forward. The others gave way, moved aside, so that this one could come up to Mathers' immobile form and look down into his open eyes.

"Can he hear me, OrDjina?" this one asked, human vocabulary coming only with difficulty to his lips, mouth, and tongue.

"Yes, sir, I believe he can," OrDjina answered, a respect and a submissiveness in her voice that Eric Mathers had never heard before.

"Hear me, then, you who are known by many names. I am called Foraldar. Some call me the Inquisitor. You will know me as Master."

Through the eyes of Eric Mathers, and through his own electromagnetic vision, the Shadowy Man looked at the one who called himself Master Foraldar the Inquisitor.

He was as tall as a man, taller than Scoti, equal in height to Sol of Sol-Jodala, and, like a man, he had two arms, two legs, a head on a neck above his shoulders, two eyes, a nose, a mouth, and two ears. He looked much like a man, yet there was a coloring of blue to his skin and his eyes were too large and his jaw was hinged wrongly and he had six fingers on each hand.

"We have many names," Foraldar said slowly, carefully articulating his words to the being he believed to be Eric Mathers, who was he, but was also something more. "To you we are the masters. You will do as we say. You will obey. You will answer. And you will assist." The being glanced over his shoulder at G'lendal and said, "With your mind, speak to him. Tell him why we have come."

Foraldar stepped back a pace or two to make room

for the black woman, who approached the form of Mathers, extended her fingers, and touched his temples.

In the background he could hear OrDjina's whispering voice asking of Scoti, "Who is this man?"

"He called himself Eric Mathers when I knew him," Scoti whispered in reply.

"Eric Mathers?" OrDjina said with a gasp.

"Exactly," Scoti told her.

Inside Eric Mathers' head, inside the Shadowy Man's mind, came these words: *Eric, you know me, don't you? G'lendal, G'lendal from Staunton. We have come to help you, Eric. We know what you are and we wish to help you.*

Help me? the Shadowy Man asked, pretending to be the man who was but a single part of him. *How can you help me? What do you want of me?*

Eric, we know who you are. We know about the Shadowy Man and how he is fighting the Kriths. The Kriths are our enemies too. Together we can fight them and together we can defeat them.

Exactly who are you asking me to help? That thing over there?

He is not a thing, Eric. You would never give them a chance to explain themselves. They aren't our enemies. They're helping us fight the Kriths. They and mankind, together with you, can defeat the Kriths.

And then be what, G'lendal? A race of lapdogs for your masters?

That's just Foraldar's way of speaking, Eric. He's our leader, our unit's leader, and like any good leader he expects his people to follow his orders.

It sounds like a great deal more than that to me.

You don't understand, Eric. . . .

I don't even want to understand the mentality of a willing slave, G'lendal.

Eric! That's not the way it is at all.

Isn't it? Then tell me, G'lendal, what is he? What

kind of creatures are they and where do they come from?

There's no time for all that now, Eric. We will explain it to you later, when it's safe. . . .

While this mental conversation passed back and forth, the Shadowy Man formed a second mental extension, a fine and delicate psionic probe, which he carefully pushed toward the creature who called himself Master Foraldar, toward the brightly glowing point of alien mental light in the psionic darkness.

He probed, touched, entered into the brightness, and found . . .

Even the Shadowy Man, a composite of 337 human cerebral cortices and their mentation patterns, who had entered into the minds of parallel Eric Matherses and who had grappled with the minds of the female rulers of the Kriths, could not deal with what he now encountered: below the glow of self-awareness, of consciousness, he found inside the mind of Foraldar a type of mental process such as he had never encountered before, had never even imagined. This was not a mind like a man's, or even like a Krith's, or like that of the composite Tromas, or even, by a stretch of the imagination, a mind like that of an electronic computer. There were mental processes going on there, passages of neural impulses, thoughts being created, but these were being done in fashions totally incomprehensible to the Shadowy Man. He found no way to equate these with his own mental processes, no way to translate these into anything he could understand. He could have called them dark, evil, alien, malignant, but he was not certain that would have been correct. Different, they were. Alien, yes. But beyond that he could gather almost nothing.

He formed words in the language Foraldar had spoken, pushed them into the alien mind: *What are you?*

The alien screamed, threw himself backward, clawed

at his face, then collapsed to the floor in a shuddering bundle.

The humans stood for a moment, transfixed. Then Scoti moved, turned away from the sobbing alien, faced the form of Eric Mathers, leveled his pistol, and asked, "G'lendal, what happened?"

"I don't know," the black girl said aloud, then turned back to Mathers and touched his temples again. *Eric, what have you done? . . .*

I just asked him who he was.

My God! . . . G'lendal's mind gasped. Then she said, angrily, *Leave him alone, Eric. Give us time. . . .* Aloud she said to Scoti, "He'll be okay in a minute. Get him outside and give him some water. Sol-Jodala can tend to him."

"G'lendal," Scoti cried, "we're running out of time."

"I know," she said, glancing back at Mathers. "But give me just a few more minutes. I've got to convince him."

"Maybe it would be better to kill him now," Scoti said.

"Foraldar wants him."

"Wanted him, you mean. He may be ready to kill him now too."

"Then he will have to decide that," G'lendal said. "See to him."

Angrily, reluctantly, with the help of the physician Sol-Jodala, Scoti carried Foraldar out of the room and into the corridor.

Well, Eric, G'lendal said into his mind, *do you see what you have done?*

It wasn't my intention to harm him.

You did, though. Their minds are very unlike ours, although I am surprised that even you have the power to cause him pain like that.

I've changed a lot since you knew me. . . .

I know that. That's why we're here.

Why?

As I said, we know of the Shadowy Man. We need him.

You won't get him until I know a great deal more.

And I told you we don't have the time.

What's the hurry?

Don't be a fool, Eric. If we know of the Shadowy Man, where he is, don't you think the Kriths do too?

Yes, I suppose they would. But how did you know?

We have no time for all that now. Just think on this: if we have come here, the Kriths are surely sending people too. They will be here soon. . . .

I imagine they will, G'lendal, but it will be too late for them, just as it's too late for you.

And what do you mean by that, Eric?

Answer my questions and I'll answer yours. What is this Foraldar of yours? Where does he come from?

A mental sigh. *Oh, very well, Eric. Foraldar's people, the people you know as "Albigensians," come from a Timeline on which there occurred a terrible genetic war.*

Explain that . . .

Very well. On Foraldar's Line of origin, the Kriths returned to Earth from UR-427-51-IV, as you know, but rather than moving across the Lines and establishing KHL-000, they remained and set out to exterminate the humans of that world. During the war that followed there were—

G'lendal's narrative was cut short by the sound of shouting voices, then the firing of weapons.

"Right over there, Cal-sarlin," said the first of the voices, a deep, masculine voice speaking in Shangalis. "Over . . . Look out!"

"Who . . ."

Guns began to fire.

"Paratimers!"

G'lendal screamed.

Through Mathers' eyes the Shadowy Man could not see what was happening, divorced himself from that body, threw psionic extensions into the corridor, then saw.

A band of men, led by a towering, naked, ugly Krith, was coming down the corridor, armed as were the Paratimers. The two men leading the Timeliners were tall and were dressed in harsh, black uniforms, and they had sighted the Paratimers outside the room clustering around the figure of Foraldar, had yelled a warning to their Krithian leader. Scoti had gotten his weapon up and had pulled off the first shot. As they dispersed, the Timeliners fired back.

Now energy weapons and slug throwers raked the hallway. A blast of coherent energy caught the kneeling Scoti full in the face, washed away flesh to blackened bone, kicked Scoti's still-writhing body backward against a wall. Leaden slugs tore through both members of the telepathic team Sol-Jodala, ripping apart Sol's arm and shoulder, almost cutting Jodala apart at the waist. Another bundle of slugs kicked into the still-prostrate Foraldar, puncturing his green uniform and the body wearing it, giving it some semblance of jerking life as the impact of the slugs knocked him against the crumpling form of Scoti.

OrDjina, who had been standing in the doorway, leaped back into the recording room, too frightened even to use the gun she held. G'lendal stood transfixed.

In moments the two black-clad men stood in the doorway, their energy pistols covering the two women and the immobile Eric Mathers.

The Shadowy Man recognized the towering men dressed in midnight black, Turothians, Eric Mathers had once heard them called. Humans, but . . . from worlds so far across the Timelines, the products of experiences so far outside the pale of Eric Mathers, that it had been hard for him to consider them humans.

One was named Pall, and the look he gave Mathers was one of intense hatred.

The second was named Marth, and he had but one

hand, and the look that he gave Mathers was of even greater hatred.

Both their energy pistols were now leveled at the motionless form, at Eric Mathers' chest, and it would have taken only a few ounces of pull on the weapons' triggers to reduce this corporeal body to charred organic ruin.

Neither of the men spoke.

Next into the room came the Krith, a tall, sable-colored being Mathers had known by the name Cal-sarlin, a minister to the Tromas back on KHL-000. He was naked, as his kind almost always were, and he smiled.

"Good afternoon, ladies," he said in the French-descended language of the Paratimers. OrDjina let her pistol fall from limp fingers. G'lendal now began to come out of her shock, though she looked at the Krith with incredulity. "And good afternoon to you, Eric." He smiled wickedly. "I can only say that I am glad we have caught you again—and saved you from your Paratimer friends. This time, well, we shall see that you do not escape us again."

Outside, in the corridor, above the four ruined corpses, now stood a stocky, redheaded man who could have been a caricature of an Irishman, but was anything but that. Mathers had known him by the name Kjemi Stov. And if there was hatred on his face, it was well hidden by a noncommittal look of Timeliner efficiency.

Cal-sarlin glanced over his shoulder toward Stov.

"Shall I go on?" the red-haired man asked in Shangalis.

"You know where they are, I believe," the Krith replied in the same language. "See that they are all destroyed."

Stov nodded curtly and went off down the hallway, and as he did so the Shadowy Man saw that he led half a dozen almost-men, Mager-types in dark, harsh uniforms, and each of them carried an automatic weapon.

"I regret what happened to your friends, ladies," Cal-sarlin said politely in the language of the Paratimers. "But they did present us something of a problem. If you can see your way clearly to cooperate with us, no harm will come to you."

OrDjina spoke an obscenity, then spit on the floor near the Krith's unshod feet.

G'lendal merely looked at the Krith's brown, marble-round eyes. Her face was devoid of expression, though there may have been hatred in her eyes.

"We do not customarily persecute women," Cal-sarlin told them. "But you must consider yourselves prisoners of war and conduct yourselves accordingly."

OrDjina repeated herself. G'lendal did nothing.

"And as for you, friend Eric," the Krith said carefully, "we are not yet certain what you are, or what you have become. Given time, the Tromas will be able to determine that, I am certain. But that will be after the fact, I am afraid. A postmortem, shall we say?"

He stepped closer to the motionless figure. The two Turothians, Pall and Marth, flanked him, the aim of their weapons never faltering.

"I know you can hear me, Eric," Cal-sarlin said, switching to Shangalis. "The Tromas at least know your physical condition and its relationship to your, ah, replicates. We will see to them. And to you."

He paused, ruminated, scratched himself, then said, "We do not think you can harm us, either you or your Shadowy Man. But even if you could, it would be useless. More of us will come here—are coming here already. So, if we fail, Eric, others who follow us will not fail.

"I do wish we had more time to speak with you, Eric, but . . ."

The Krith's voice was interrupted by the remote

chattering of automatic weapons, the sounds of shattering glass and spilling liquids.

"Your replicates, you know," Cal-sarlin said. "Pall, Marth, you may now see to his . . ."

Even while the fingers of the black-clad men were pulling back on triggers, the Shadowy Man felt himself dying, dissolving, disrupting as leaden slugs tore through the bodies of his replicates, felt the horrible agonies of their dying, a prelude to his own. . . .

One of the fourteen-year-old bodies was all but cut in half, its entrails spilling out, wet and bloody, through gashes in its abdomen. A huge, jagged sliver of glass tore into the chest of another replicate, slashing into heart and lungs as nutrient fluid, now reddened with blood, spilled out of the shattered encanter. A bullet pierced the eye of a third replicate, stunning it but not yet killing it, throwing it against the back of the cylinder, which shattered with the impact, impaling the body on stalagmites of glass. . . .

As the triggers of the Turothians' energy weapons completed their travel and electrical circuits closed inside the weapons, the Shadowy Man began what he knew to be the last act of his existence.

Psionic fingers grasped the fabric of space/time that surrounded the physical form of Eric Mathers, tightened, pulled, jerked, flexed, tore, retreated. One last parachronal convolution was opening, one last spot of blackness swelling to encompass the man who soon would be all that was left of the Shadowy Man.

He pulled the bubble out of its context, still not fully understanding how he was doing it, but knowing that he was doing it. The bubble crossed the nothingness of everything, touched another strand of space/time, and joined the convolution through which the skudder had recently gone. He released his grip on the bubble, left it to fall, twist, spin, and snap through the joined convolutions across time and space and paratime to the Far World. Eric Mathers was safe, as safe as he could be in a universe about to undergo cataclysmic reorganization.

Then he flickered his dying awareness back into the Underground, back to where enough replicates still lived to sustain some portion of himself, back to where the Krith and the two black-clad men and the two women who had worked for the Paratimers now stood, all in dumbfounded astonishment as they struggled with the after-effects of the implosion caused by the sudden disappearance of the physical matter of Eric Mathers' body. The sphere of blackness had appeared and then vanished so quickly that none of them could have really seen it.

"Damn you!" Cal-sarlin cried as he picked himself up off the floor, his Krithian dignity hurt more than anything else. "Damn you, Eric Mathers, damn you . . ."

Pall and Marth looked at each other with incomprehension on their faces. Their energy blasts had done nothing but sear the far wall.

The implosion had ripped OrDjina's thin gown, half torn it from her body, but she hardly seemed aware that her breasts were exposed and her beautiful coiffure destroyed. Her face showed only fear.

Against the console that housed the still-operating mnemonic recorder leaned G'lendal, gasping for breath, but on her face there was a tiny smile, as if she understood better than any of the others what had happened, and her smile was given to the common enemy of the Kriths and the Paratimers, who was winning this very last battle of them all.

Although his strength was fading rapidly, his existence winking out as replicate after replicate died under the bullets of Kjemi Stov and the Magers, the Shadowy Man found the strength within what was left of himself to make the air speak one last time.

"Cal-sarlin," said the voice out of the air, the voice of Eric Mathers, "we have come to the end of the road, all of us. There is not the strength within me now to tell you all of it, so this will have to do: you and your kind, and the Paratimers too, all of you have lost, lost now and forever. Tell your Tromas that. If there is still time."

Fear now replaced incomprehension on the Krith's face. His voice was weak and faltering when he said, "W-what do you mean?"

"The end of the world is at hand," the Shadowy Man said, and laughed, and died.

G'lendal laughed with him, a laughter that bordered on hysteria.

OrDjina screamed.

Cal-sarlin's hands made and then unmade fists. But he never had the time to begin to comprehend the meaning of the Shadowy Man's last words.

The reorganization of the universe had already begun. And in moments there was not/never would be any such thing as a Krith.

It was 14:07:21, 4 March 1973.

23
The Far World

It was morning, 15 January 1972, as time is recorded on some worlds, when I awoke and found out who I was.

Even as I started to pull myself to my knees and rise enough to observe my surroundings, once again wholly and only Eric Mathers, I was struck by an appalling sense of loss, a terrible poignancy, and a realization of my own human limitations. I, who had once been a part of the Shadowy Man—or would be, if you want to look at time that way—was now just a man again, and after the experience through which I had just passed, that didn't seem like a great deal to be: human and so terribly finite.

From my knees I finally drew myself to my feet, pulling myself up with my hands around the trunk of a slender, graceful tree, something a bit like a willow, which grew beside a small, quickly flowing stream. A breeze moved along with the stream, across my naked hips, and I realized that I had arrived there, wherever *there* was, without clothing. And this realization came too: I had arrived without the chair I had been in, without the straps that had held me in the chair while drugged. Somehow the Shadowy Man had discarded them along the way, along with my clothing. I silently thanked him for getting me out of the Underground alive and well, and found my eyes moving toward the sky, as if now I identified *him* with some sort of heavenly deity. But I knew he hadn't been that. Less than a god. But, if he'd had the time . . .

It was a morning sky that was above me. Somehow

I was certain of that. A clear blue sky with wispy patches of clouds here and there. In my nudity the sun was comfortably warm.

Around me were forest and meadow. Graceful, thin-leafed trees, not quite like any I'd ever known anywhere else, clustering clumps of grasses, scattered mushroomlike growths, some of which might have been as much as ten feet tall. Remotely, a birdlike creature sang from the limb of a tree, calling his mate or maybe marking the limits of his territory, I thought. And I now knew where I was. I'd been there before. And an earlier version of me, along with Sally, would be coming soon.

And I knew what the Shadowy Man had left for me to do. A couple of little things he hadn't been able to do himself, just to round out what *I* remembered of the past. I could do that much for him, couldn't I?

After a quick dip in the cold, clear water of the creek, I set out to do those things.

The skudder sat not far from the little stream, a few hundred feet, no more, a bright and untarnished craft, the product of a "future" world that would soon cease to exist, *soon* being March of next year. The skudder wouldn't be built until years after that, but that didn't matter. Until next March that future would exist, at least in potentiality, and for now that was enough for me. If the Shadowy Man hadn't been able to fully understand Time, how could I ever hope to?

I went into the skudder he had delivered there, and for a moment sat before the controls, wondering what would happen if I were to start it up and in it leave this world. What would have become of that other Eric Mathers if he had had no skudder? How could he ever have gone to the world of the BrathelLanza and become the Shadowy Man? But then, would it even be possible for me to use the skudder if I wanted to? Possibly. Probably. For this is a universe of probabilities, never of certainties.

Inside one of the skudder's lockers I found clothing, and dressed, and then had myself a quick meal from the skudder's provisions, which were decidedly better than skudder fare usually is.

As I ate, I thought: Some distance to the west of where the skudder sat was a small, rather primitive village inhabited by people who could have been called civilized. The village was on the frontier of a small kingdom of people who were just beginning to work iron into weapons and jewelry, the smelting of iron a newly discovered art Here and Now. Although semi-barbarians, they weren't a bad lot. I'd lived with them for a while—or I would. Sally and I hadn't been—wouldn't be—really uncomfortable there, but then they had treated us like godlings. They'd been expecting us, I remembered. And how had they known we were coming? I'd told them, I suppose. Or I was about to tell them.

The Shadowy Man was right. This business of time travel can be very confusing.

So my first order of business was to go to the village and give the people there a little speech; I knew their language, of course. I'd tell them I was an emissary of a pair of deities who would be arriving in a few days—and with an energy pistol and a couple of other gadgets from the skudder, it shouldn't be too hard for me to convince them that I was something of a god myself. Then I'd prepare them for the man and woman, dazed and battered, naked and tired, who would come into their village soon. By the time I was finished I'd have them convinced that they were about to have a major miracle occur in their hometown, something that would really put it on the map. And when the next (or first) Eric Mathers got there, with Sally along with him, there would be no problem. At least that's how it had been with Sally and *me* when I'd come here the first time.

Then, when that was done, I would go back to the skudder and compose a note for the two fugitives from the Kriths, a note to my previous self and to Sally, which would read something like this:

"Dear Eric and Sally,

"If you read this note you will have escaped from the Tromas and have found the refuge I selected for you." I would write "I," though perhaps it would have been more honest to write "he" or "the Shadowy Man." "You're safe here as long as you wish to stay." Which was true within certain limits.

Still using the first-person singular, I would go on to say:

"I know you're curious about your means of transportation from KHL-000 to here, and I would explain it to you if I could, but none of us has the proper mathematical background to really understand it." Which was very true. I certainly didn't understand it. "I could tell you it's a 'parachronal convolution,' but what would that explain? Labeling something doesn't necessarily define it.

"This skudder, from some decades into the future, as you two have been reckoning time, is yours. It's fully provisioned and ready to take you wherever you might wish to go, spatially or paratemporally. You may use it when you will.

"Some miles to the west of here you will find a village. It is an outpost of a kingdom barely out of the Bronze Age, though its inhabitants are friendly and pleasant people. You will find yourselves welcome there, though don't be too surprised if you're treated as something a bit more special than a pair of naked wanderers. They're expecting a couple of exiled godlings. Try to act the part.

"In time you're a few weeks downtime from our recent conflict with the Tromas. In the past, as you see it.

"In space, you're still in North America, the Florida peninsula.

"In paratime, well, you're one hell of a long way to

the T-East, far beyond the Line the Kriths call KHL-000. It's as safe a place as any you can hope for, but try not to be disturbed by the oddness of some of the things you find here. There are some aspects of the evolutionary process that have worked out differently here."

I'll say! Ten-foot-tall mushrooms and fat unicorns!

But I would scribble on, and finally conclude with something like:

"As for advice, I can give you none, as much as I would like to." That was true.

"The future is yours to do with as you wish.

"I think." And that was a kind of truth too.

"Yours"—and I would sign my own name—"Eric Mathers."

That's the note I would write, but first I had a couple of other things to do.

From the skudder's locker I got several packages of provisions, took them to a place near the stream, and placed them in a small, neat pile where they were sure to be found by the two I knew were coming. If some animal didn't get them first. But I was certain they'd be waiting for Eric and Sally when they got there. I remembered them having been.

Then, feeling much better than I could remember having felt in a long, long time, I set out toward the west, where there was supposed to be—would be! I'd been there—a village that would give Eric and Sally a warm reception.

And as I walked I thought about the things that the Shadowy Man had experienced, the inexplicable paradoxes of a probabilistic universe. Nothing really *was*. Everything was just *might be*. Maybe that was a hell of a way to run a railroad, but it did keep things interesting.

And I wondered what the universe would be like *afterward,* when there were no Kriths or Timeliners or Paratimers to foul things up even worse than human beings fouled things up. Things might not be so bad. Maybe . . .

And I made a few plans of my own. After I got finished at the village and wrote my note, then I'd go off by myself for a while, do a little wandering, see the country, maybe finally get my mind together and try to understand a little of it. Then, in a few months, in late April, I'd go back to Sally and tell her what had happened. To her I'd have been gone only a few days; to me it would be more than a year.

Then . . .

Well, I wasn't certain then. I'd come back to her in April 1972, and the reorganization of the universe wasn't scheduled to happen until March 1973. We'd have almost a year to do whatever we wanted, to eat and make love and sing songs and recite poems and tell stories and make love . . . to dream and wish and hope and . . .

And wonder about 4 March 1973.

That day would come eventually.

We'd have to face it.

The Shadowy Man hadn't been certain what would happen to us, so neither could I be. Maybe there was a chance for us, way off here in the sidelines. Maybe, somehow, when the universe reordered itself, it would miss us. Maybe we could go on and have those babies after all, and be the godlings the people here thought us to be. There would be a lot of things we could do to help these people: introduce them to the concept of sanitation, tell them their world wasn't the center of the universe and help them develop this world's first constitutional monarchy. There was a lot we could do. Like the poor Timeliners used to say of themselves: they have a lot of history in front of them.

But maybe it wouldn't work out that way.

I wasn't going to be frightened about it. And I wouldn't let Sally be frightened either. Even if we did wink out of existence, come next March, it had been one hell of a life.

I wouldn't have missed it.

And as I walked toward the village, I actually felt happy.

What the hell!

I began to whistle.

And once I glanced over my shoulder in a non-direction that I imagined to be the Temporal-West and the Lines of Men, and I yelled to them:

"Good luck, you silly bastards. You're going to need it. I won't be there to help."

AUTHOR'S NOTE

The curious publishing history of *The Timeliner Trilogy* made it difficult for most readers of the hardcover editions to know where the various sequences of events began or ended.

I would like to express my thanks to Playboy Press, and especially to senior editor Sharon Jarvis, for giving the three novels that make up the trilogy this opportunity to exist as a concurrent series.

I also appreciate the opportunity given to me by Playboy Press to eliminate some of the errors, inconsistencies, and redundancies that existed in the previous editions.

And I offer a special word of thanks to Russell Galen of the Scott Meredith Literary Agency for his efforts to gain for The Timeliner Trilogy this unique existence.

To all and sundry who have helped, again, my thanks.

Richard C. Meredith
Milton, Florida
September 1978

PUBLISHER'S NOTE

Richard C. Meredith did not live to see his trilogy published. He died in March of 1979. We will miss him.